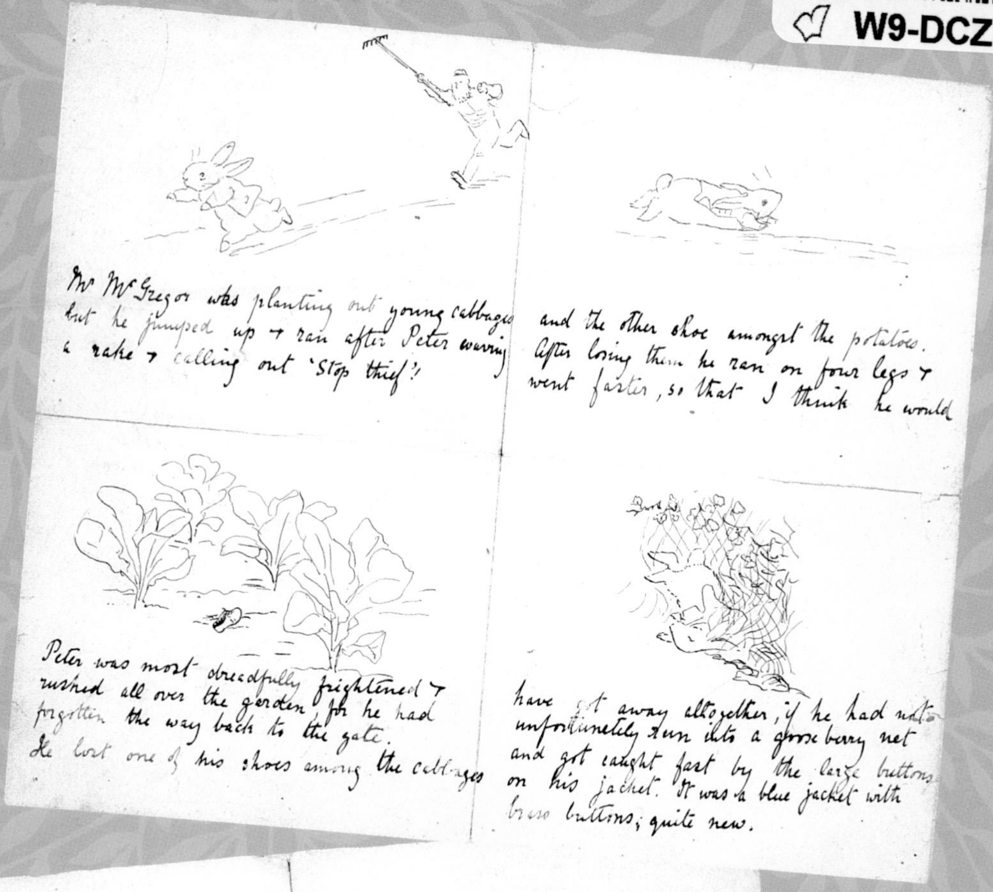

Mr McGregor was planting out young cabbages but he jumped up & ran after Peter waving a rake & calling out 'Stop thief'!

Peter was most dreadfully frightened & rushed all over the garden, for he had forgotten the way back to the gate. He lost one of his shoes among the cabbages

and the other shoe amongst the potatoes. After losing them he ran on four legs & went faster, so that I think he would

have got away altogether, if he had not unfortunately run into a gooseberry net and got caught fast by the large buttons on his jacket. It was a blue jacket with brass buttons, quite new.

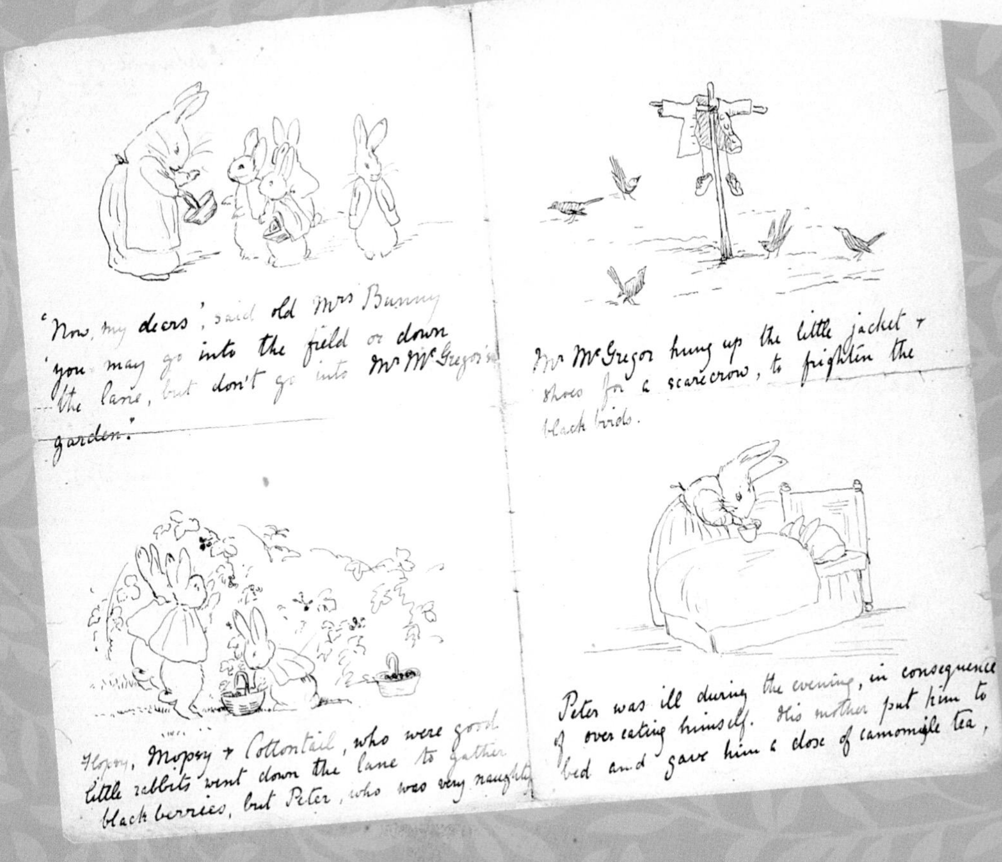

'Now, my dears', said old Mrs Bunny 'you may go into the field or down the lane, but don't go into Mr McGregor's garden.'

Flopsy, Mopsy & Cottontail, who were good little rabbits went down the lane to gather blackberries, but Peter, who was very naughty

Mr McGregor hung up the little jacket & shoes for a scarecrow, to frighten the blackbirds.

Peter was ill during the evening, in consequence of over eating himself. His mother put him to bed and gave him a dose of camomile tea,

A Note About the Endpapers

The front endpapers are a facsimile of the original picture letter sent by Beatrix Potter to Noel Moore in 1893. The back endpapers show this same letter but cleaned for greater legibility and laid out in the correct reading order.

JANE JOHNSON

My Dear Noel

The Story of a Letter from Beatrix Potter

Dial Books for Young Readers New York

For my mother

Published by Dial Books for Young Readers
A member of Penguin Putnam Inc.
375 Hudson Street • New York, New York 10014

Copyright © 1999 by Jane Johnson
All rights reserved • Designed by Nancy R. Leo
Printed in Hong Kong on acid-free paper
First Edition
1 3 5 7 9 10 8 6 4 2

Library of Congress Cataloging in Publication Data
Johnson, Jane.
My dear Noel : the story of a letter from Beatrix Potter / Jane Johnson.—1st ed.
p.   cm.
Summary: A letter from Beatrix Potter to a young friend who is ill marks
the origin of her famous tales.
ISBN 0-8037-2050-5 (tr.)—ISBN 0-8037-2051-3 (lib. bdg.)
1. Potter, Beatrix, 1866–1943—Correspondence—Juvenile literature.
2. Women authors, English—20th century—Correspondence—Juvenile literature.
3. Women artists—Great Britain—Correspondence—Juvenile literature.
4. Moore, Noel—Correspondence—Juvenile literature.
[1. Potter, Beatrix, 1866–1943. 2. Moore, Noel. 3. Letters.] I. Title.
PR6031.O72M9 1999   823'.912—dc20   [B]   96-11074   CIP   AC

The author gratefully acknowledges Judy Taylor's book Letters to Children,
published by Frederick Warne, 1992, for its invaluable information regarding the Moore family.
The art was rendered in pen-and-ink and watercolor.

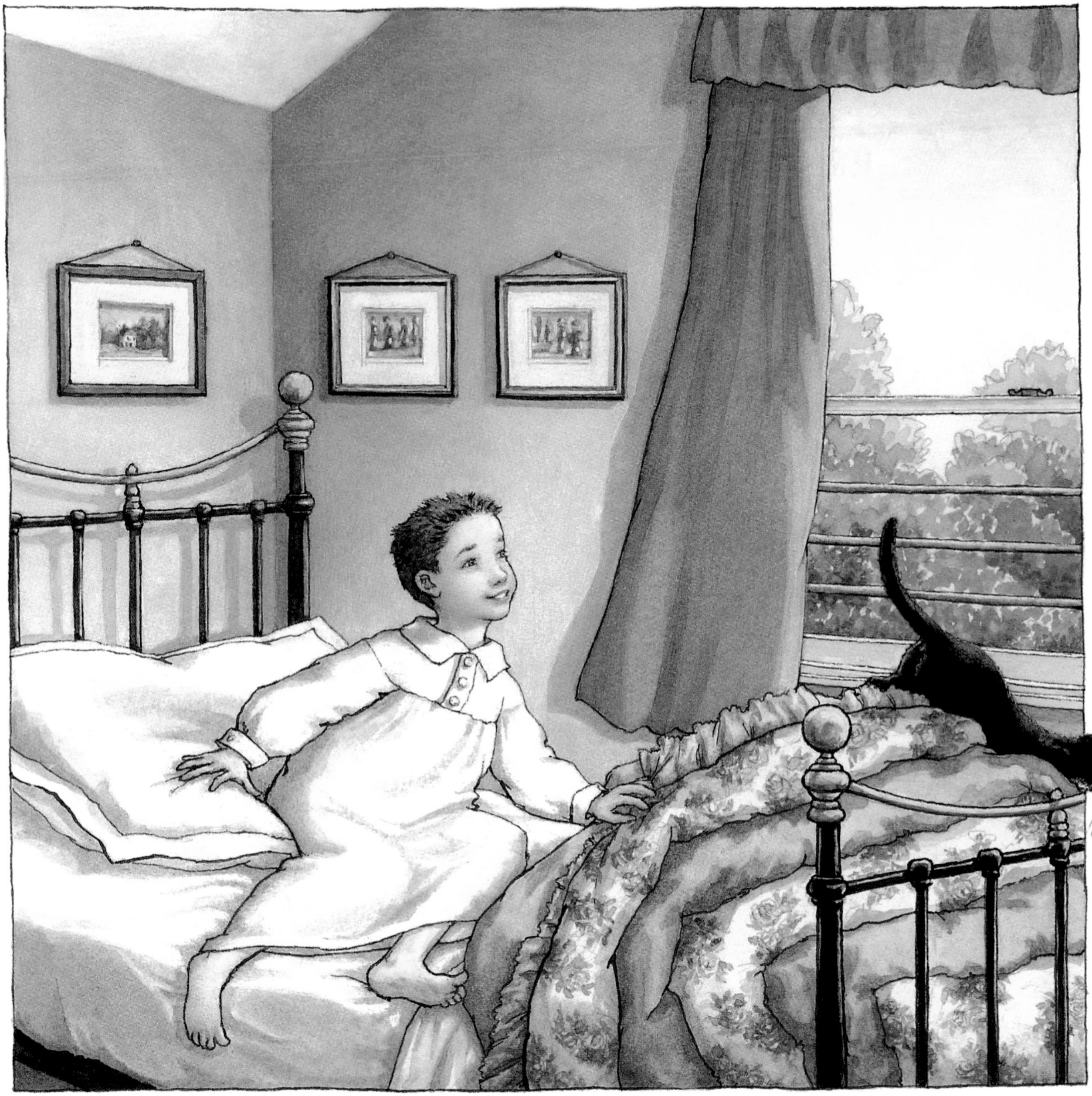

"Miss Potter's coming today!" shouted Noel as he tumbled out of bed to tell the others.

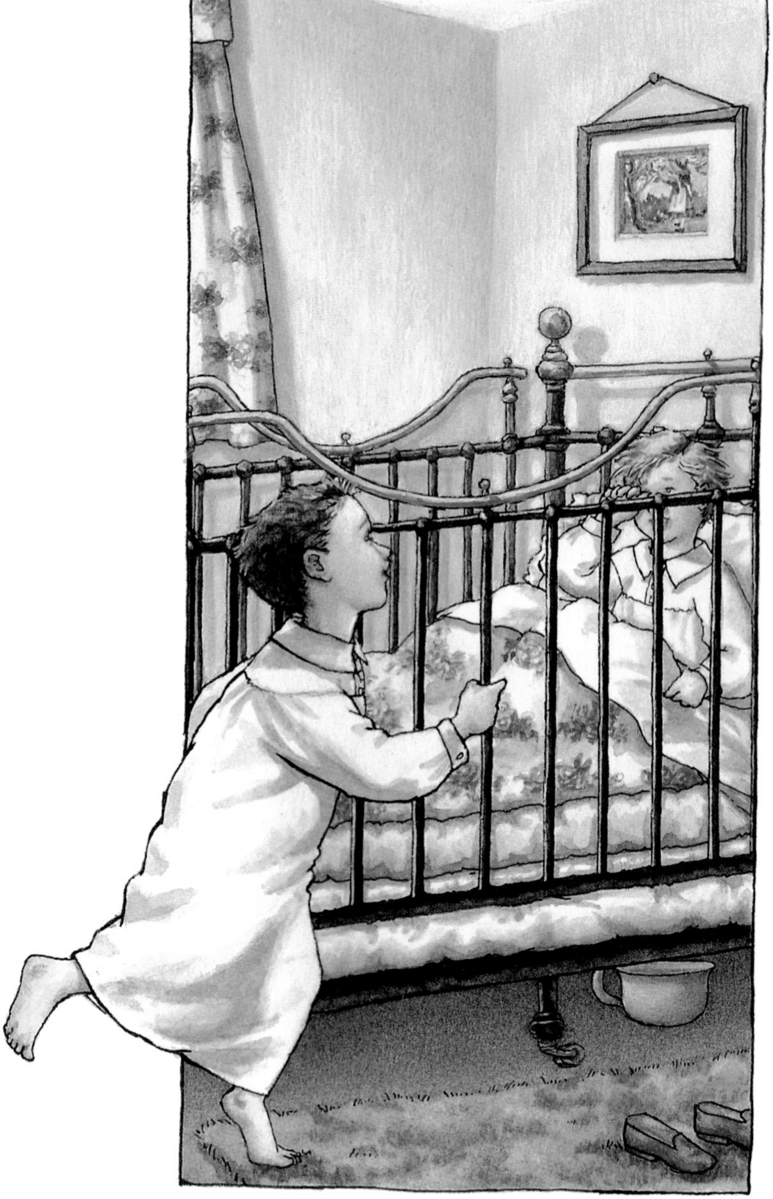 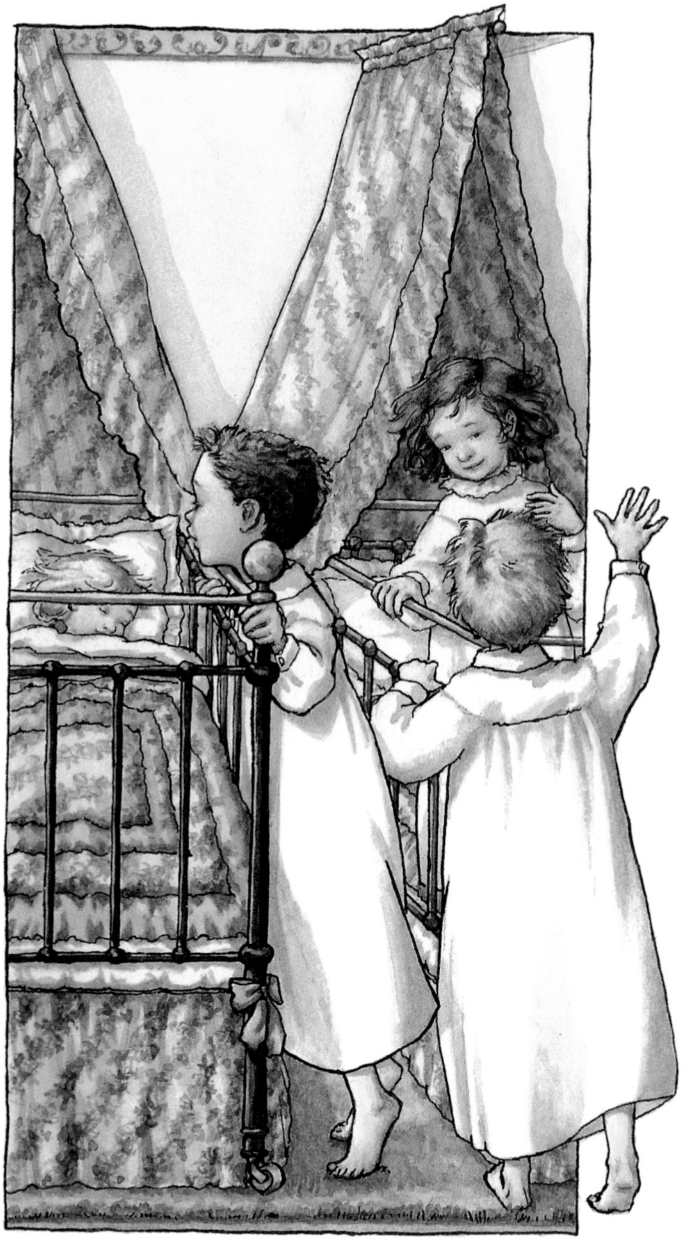

All the Moore children loved Miss Potter's visits. But Noel had known her longest, so he felt she belonged to him more than to Eric or Marjorie or Freda.

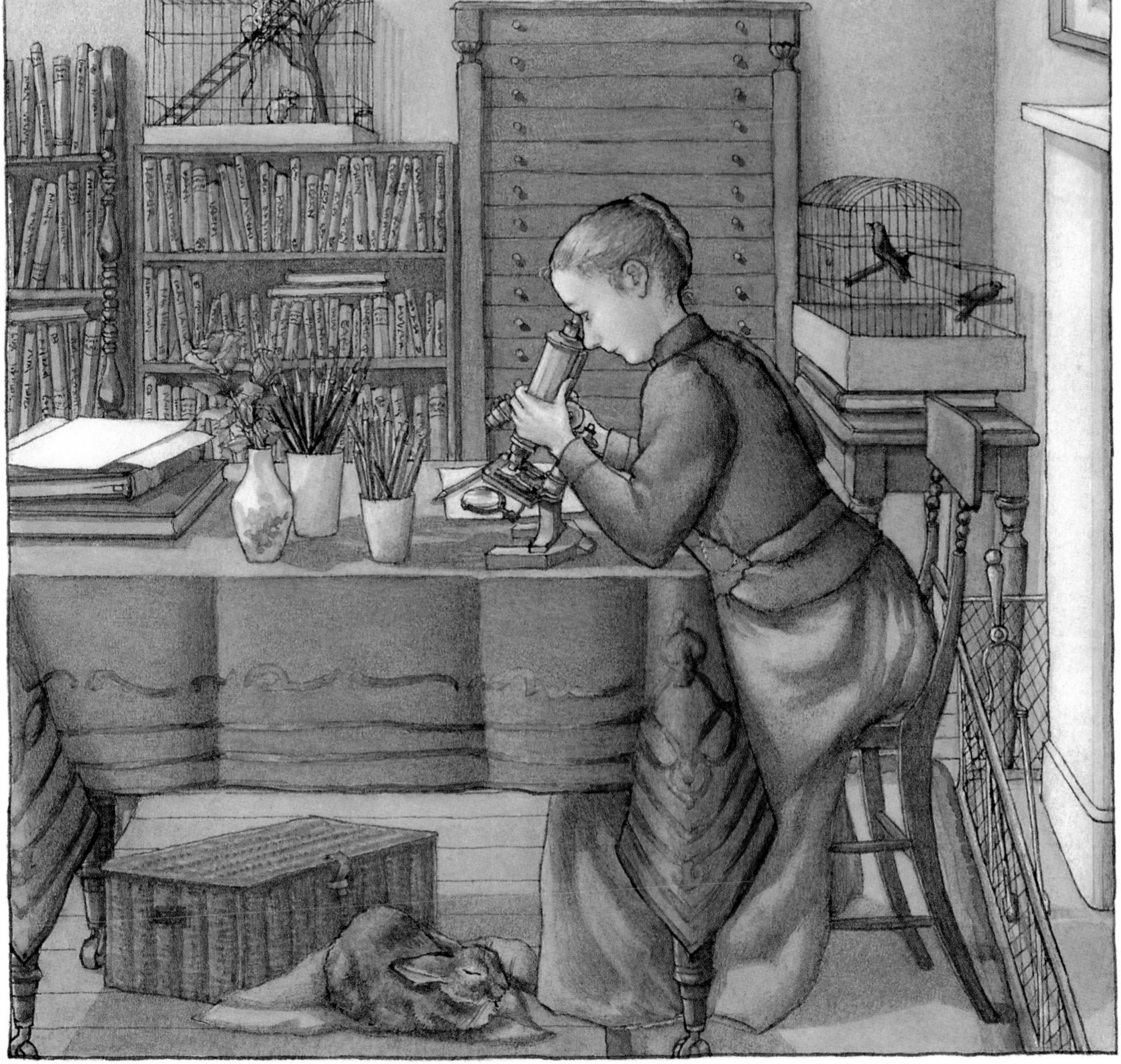

She spent so many hours alone in her room at the top of a big silent house that Noel was sure Miss Potter had much more fun with his family.

"Mama, is Miss Potter having *her* breakfast now?" Noel asked.

Before she could answer, the others began: "Will she bring her mice?" "I want to stroke her rabbit!"

"Wait and see; and don't all talk at once, dears."

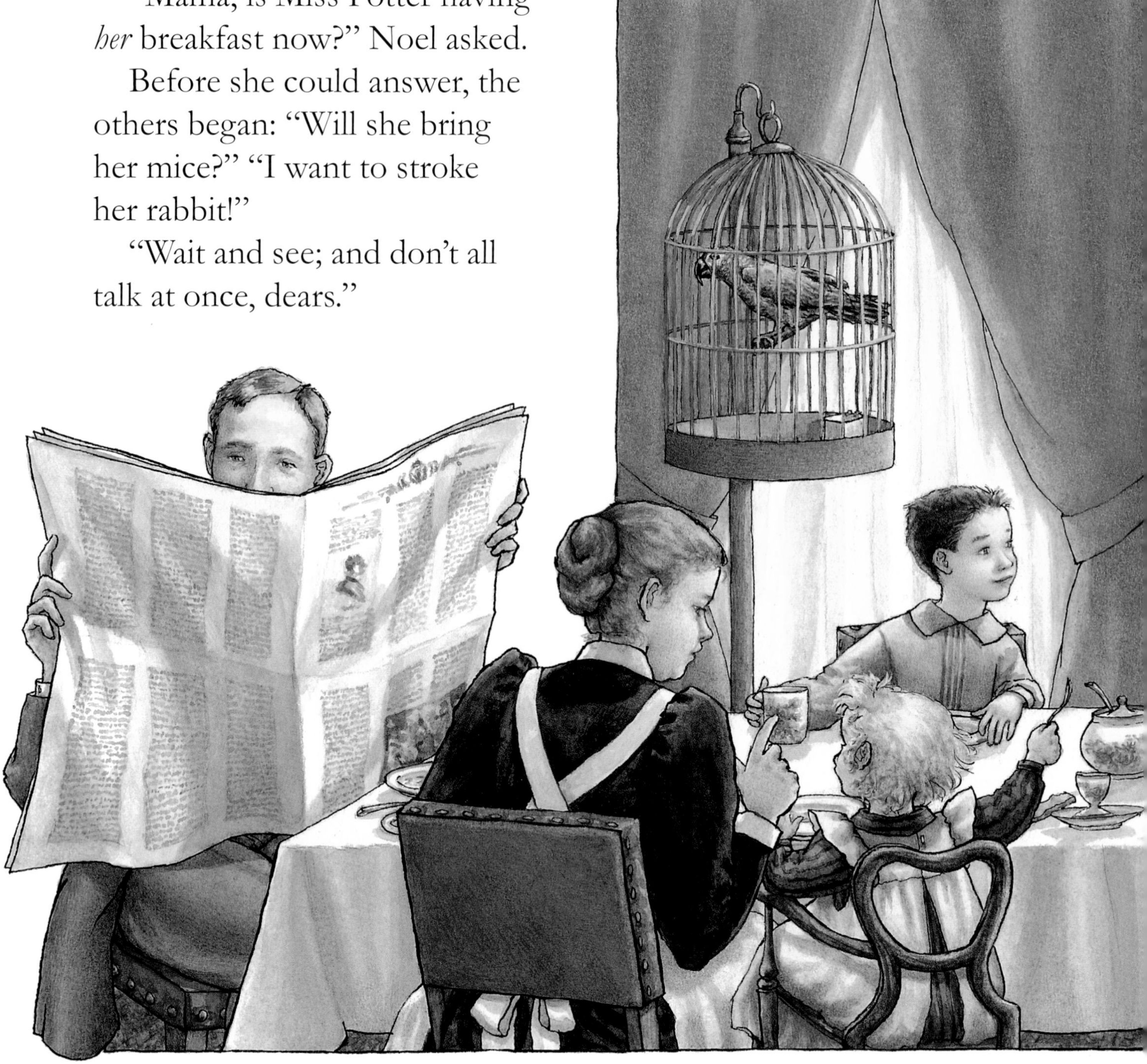

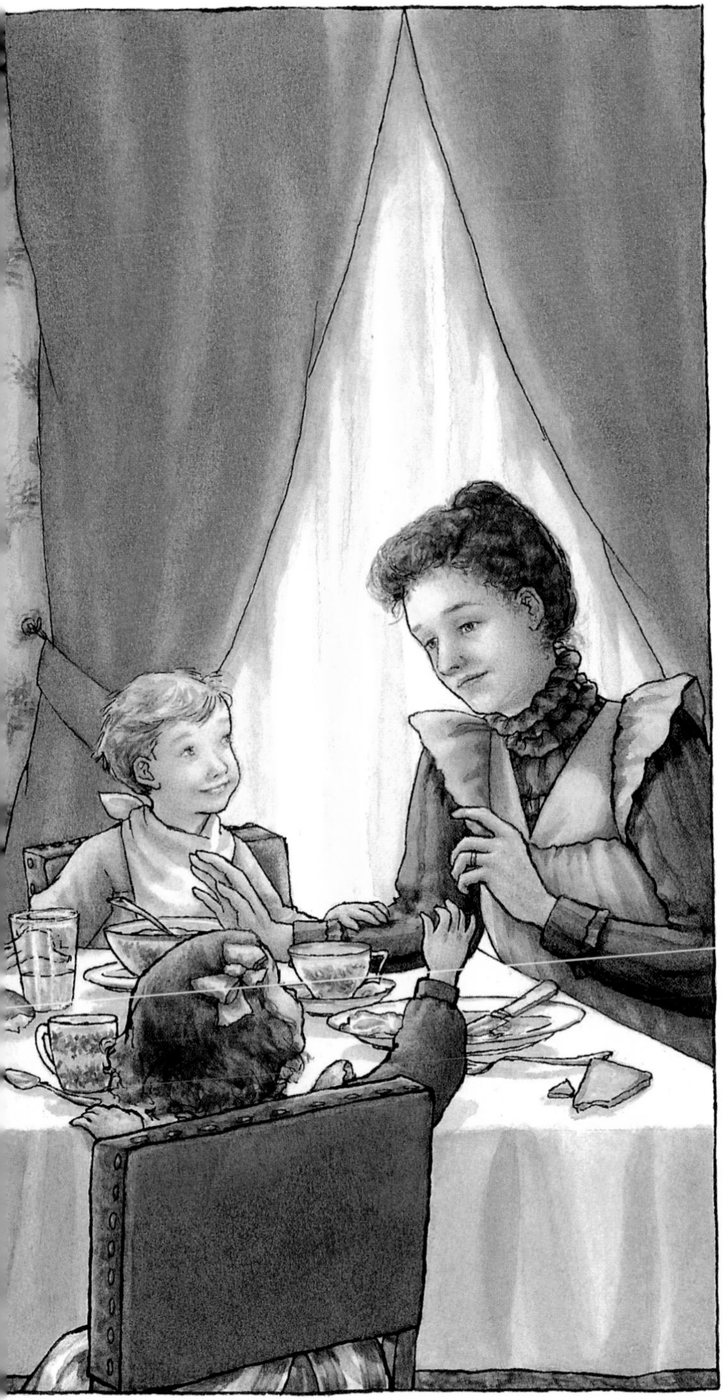
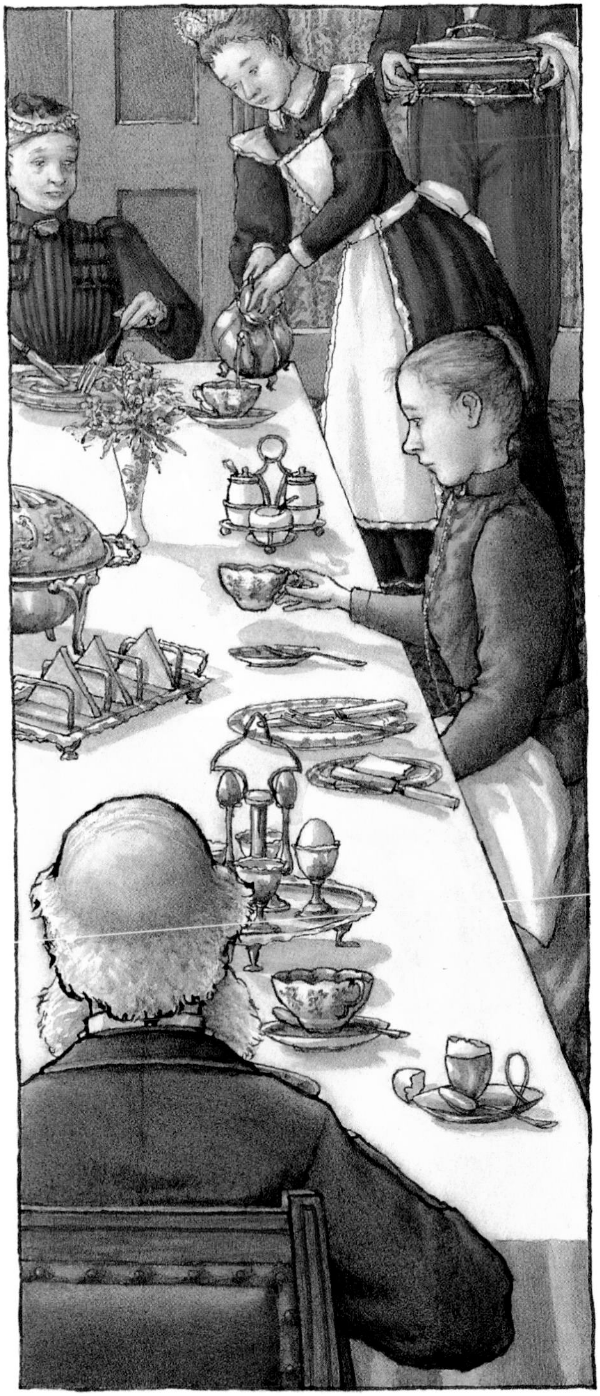

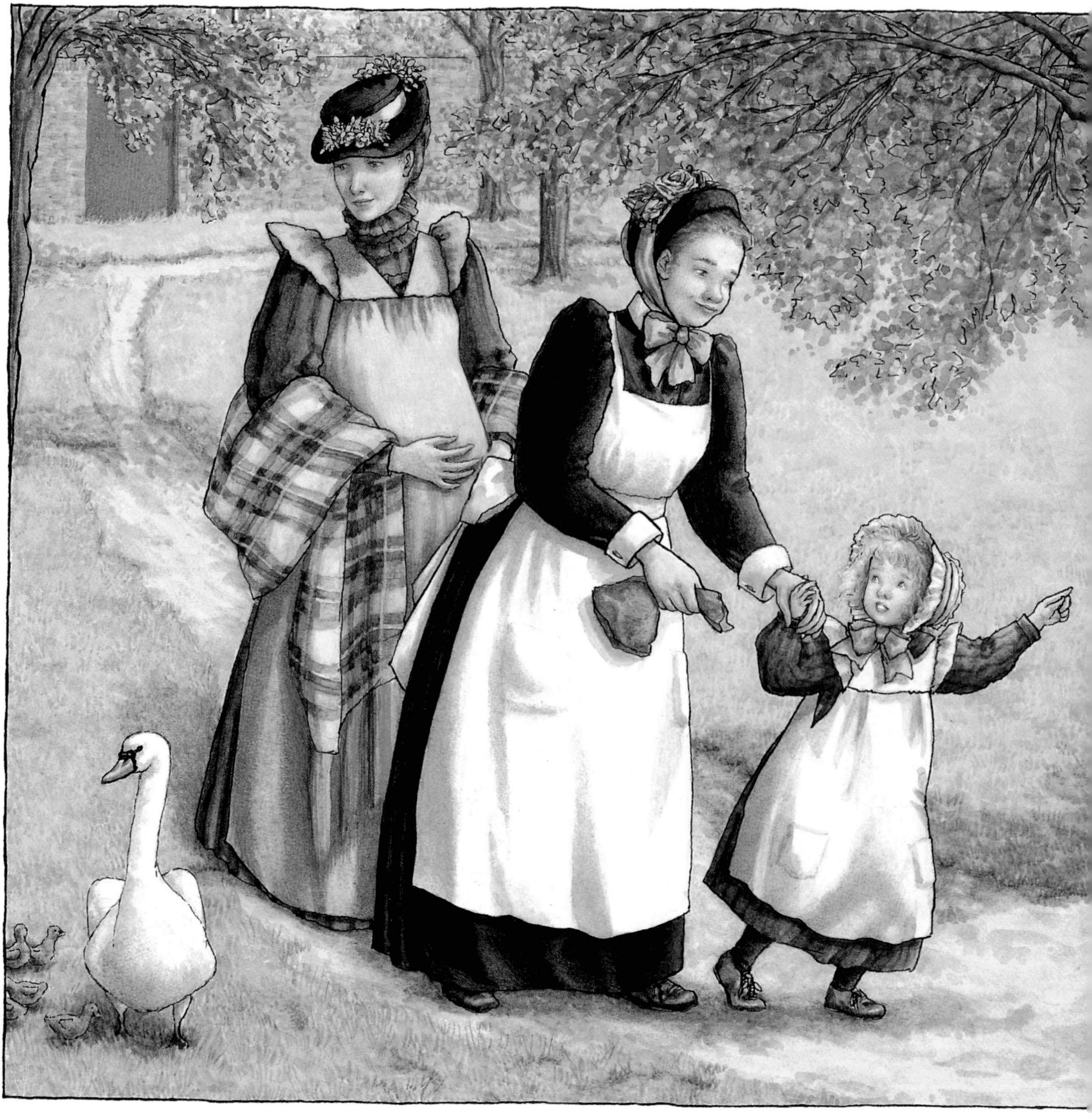

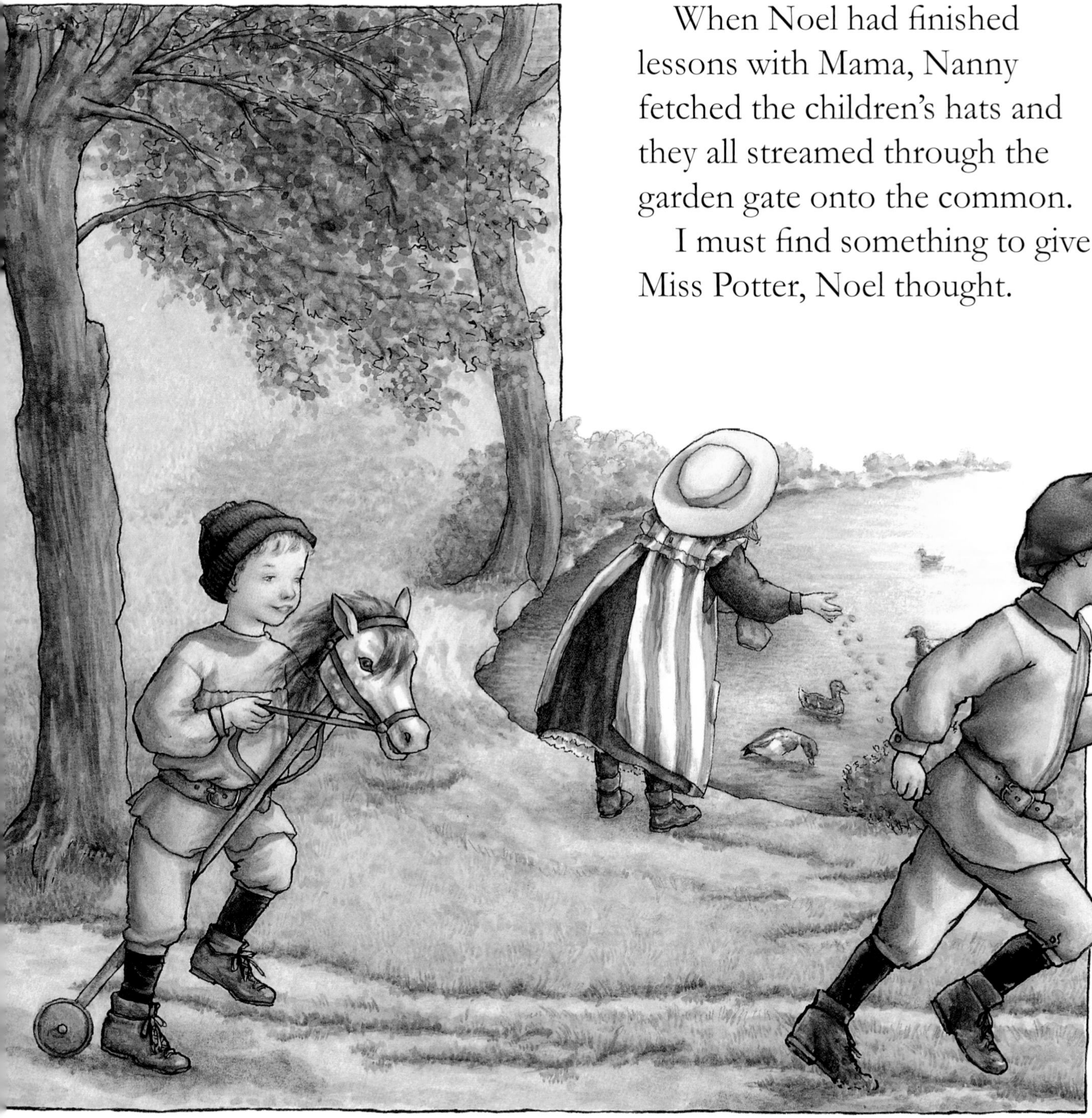

When Noel had finished lessons with Mama, Nanny fetched the children's hats and they all streamed through the garden gate onto the common.

I must find something to give Miss Potter, Noel thought.

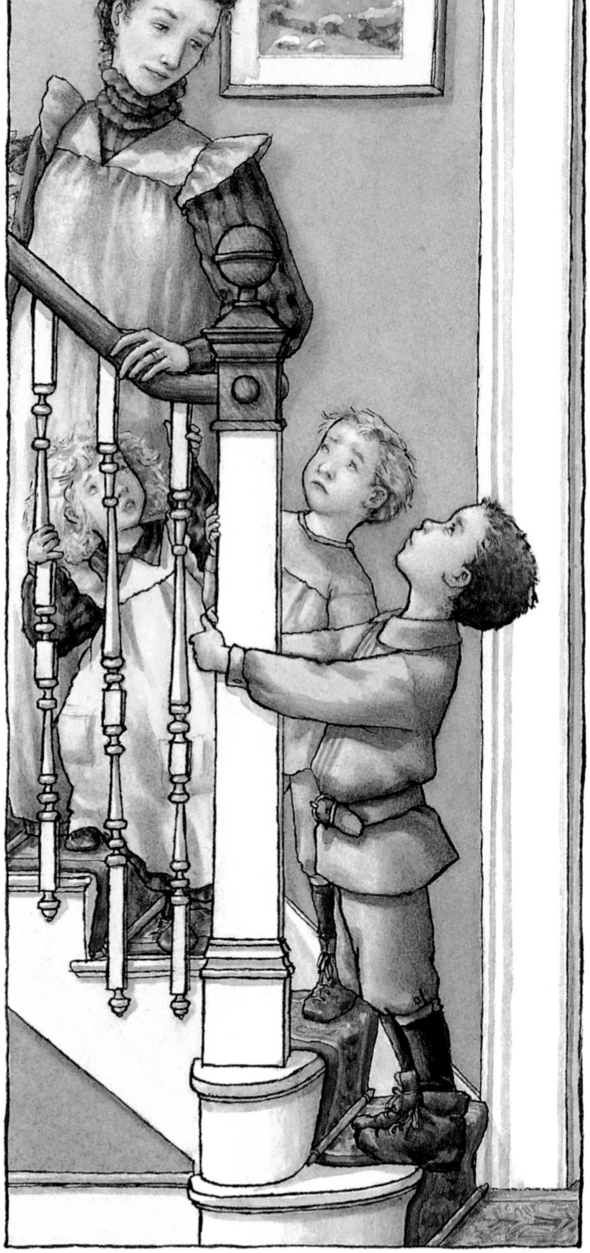

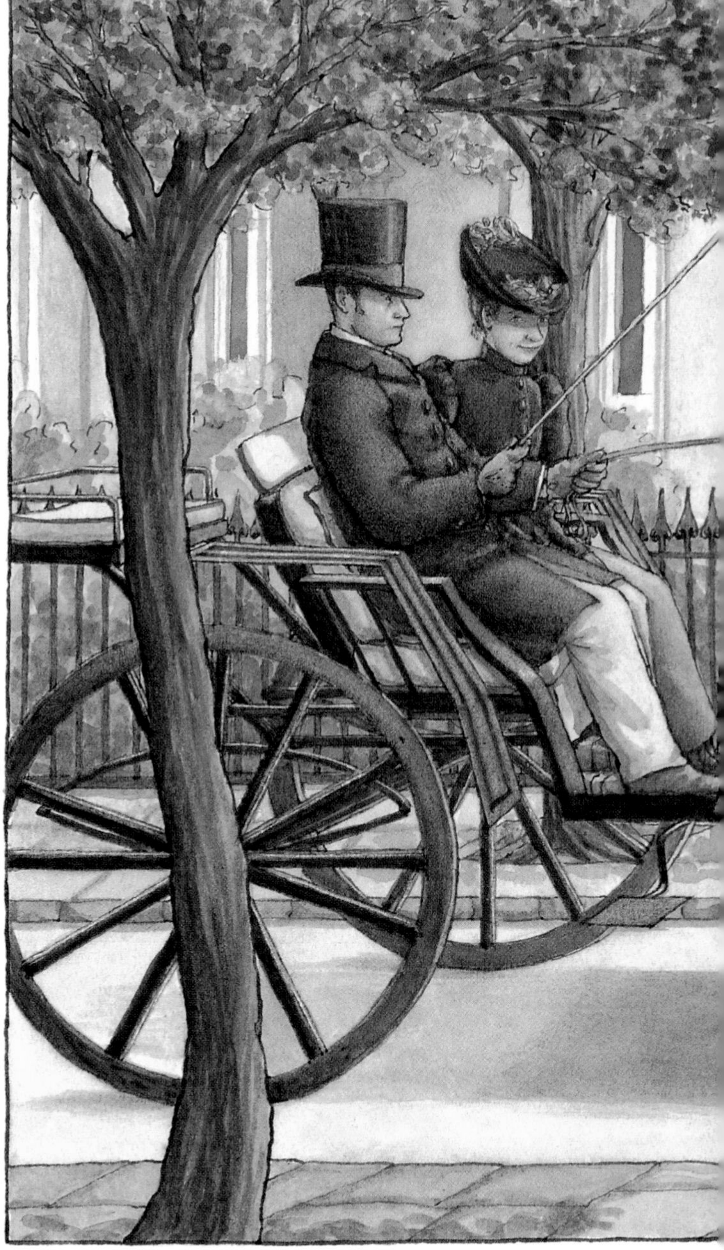

After lunch Mama said, “Now we’ll have a rest before Miss Potter comes,” and though they fussed, she bundled everyone up to bed.

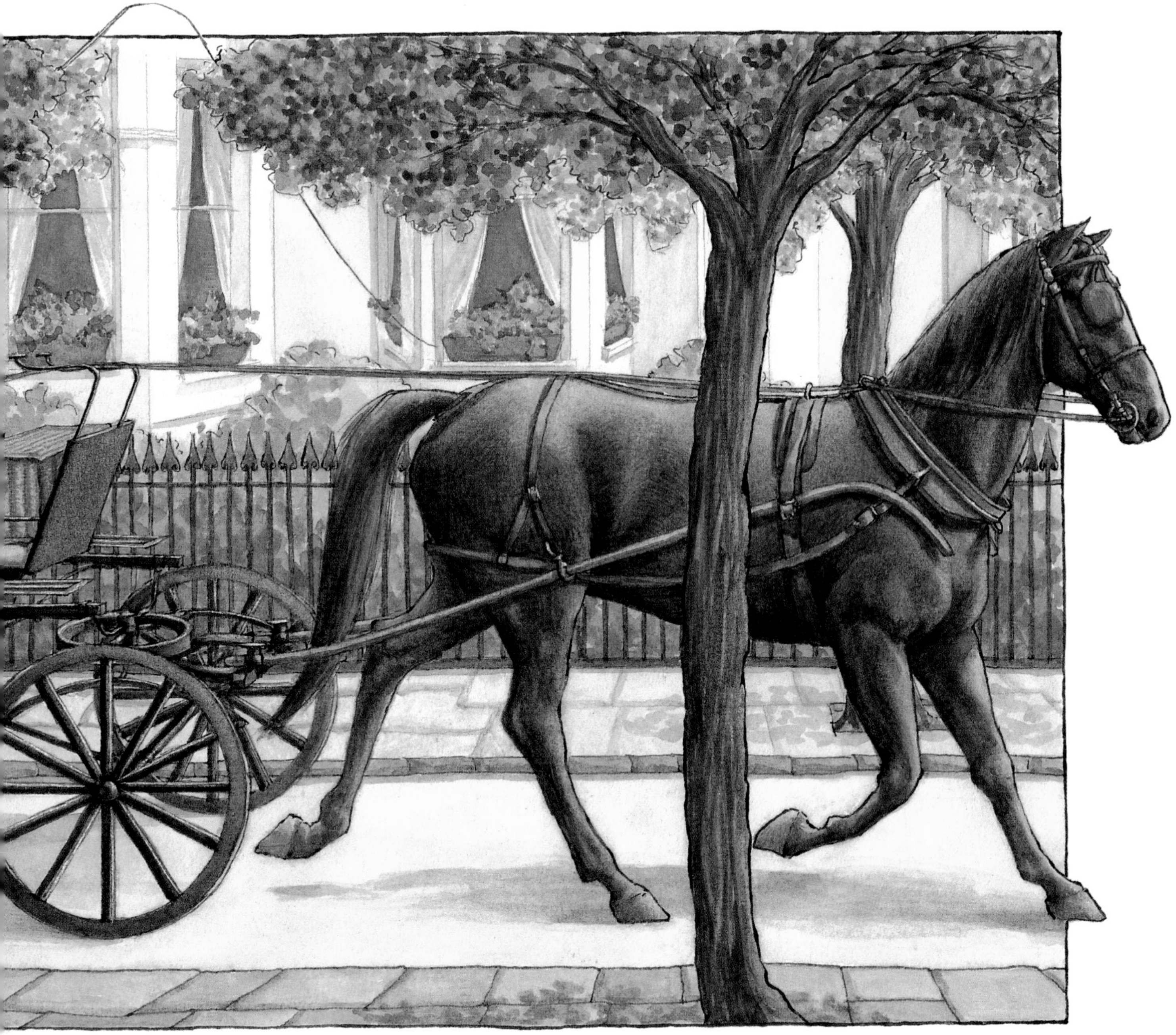

As Noel's eyes closed, he murmured, "Miss Potter's on her way."

"Oh, it's *lovely* to see all of you!" cried Miss Potter, running up the path. "Is this for me, Noel? What a wonderful color. I shall wear it in my hat."

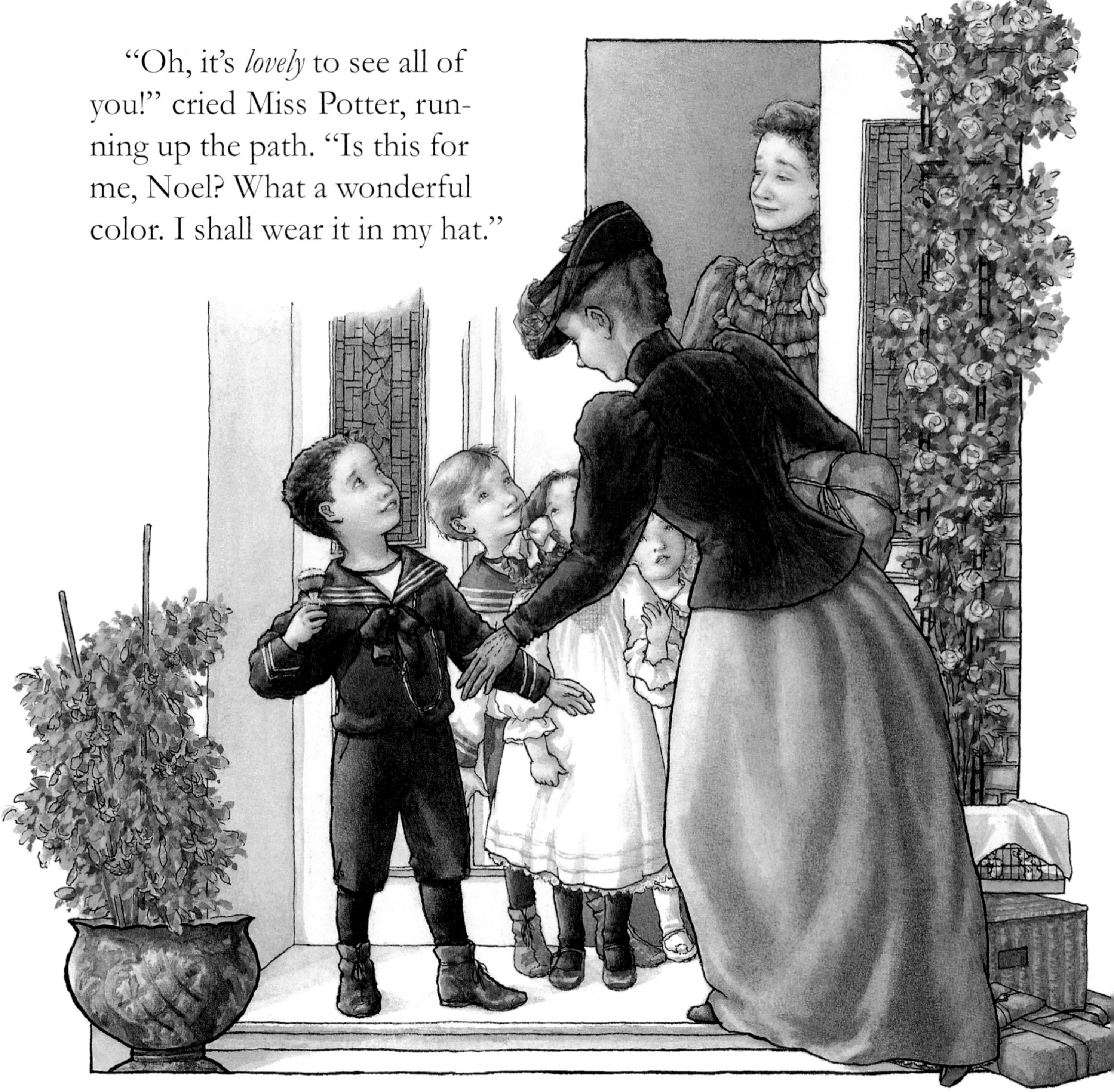

Then, opening Miss Potter's packages, they discovered treats for everyone—even the new baby who had not yet arrived.

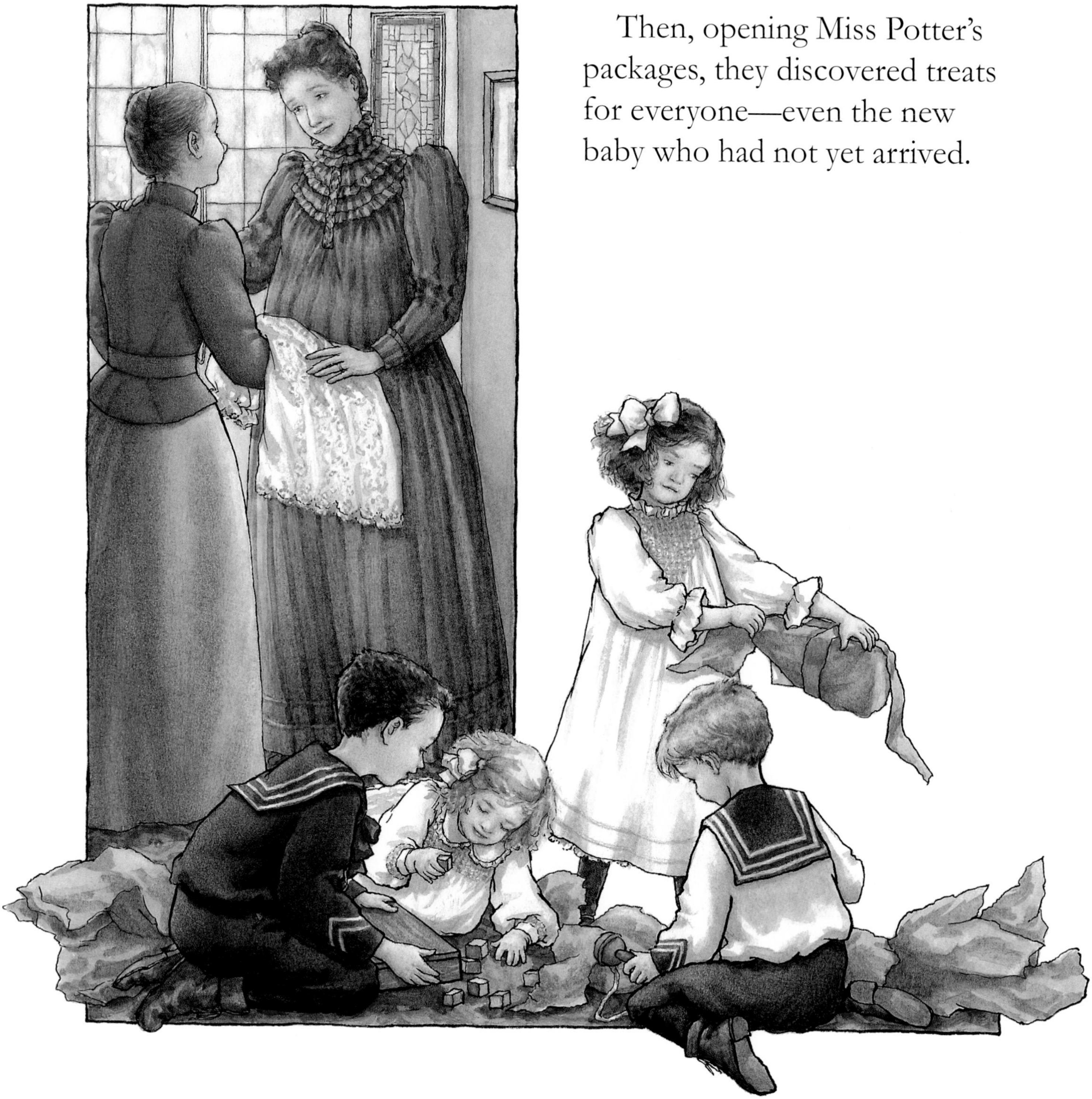

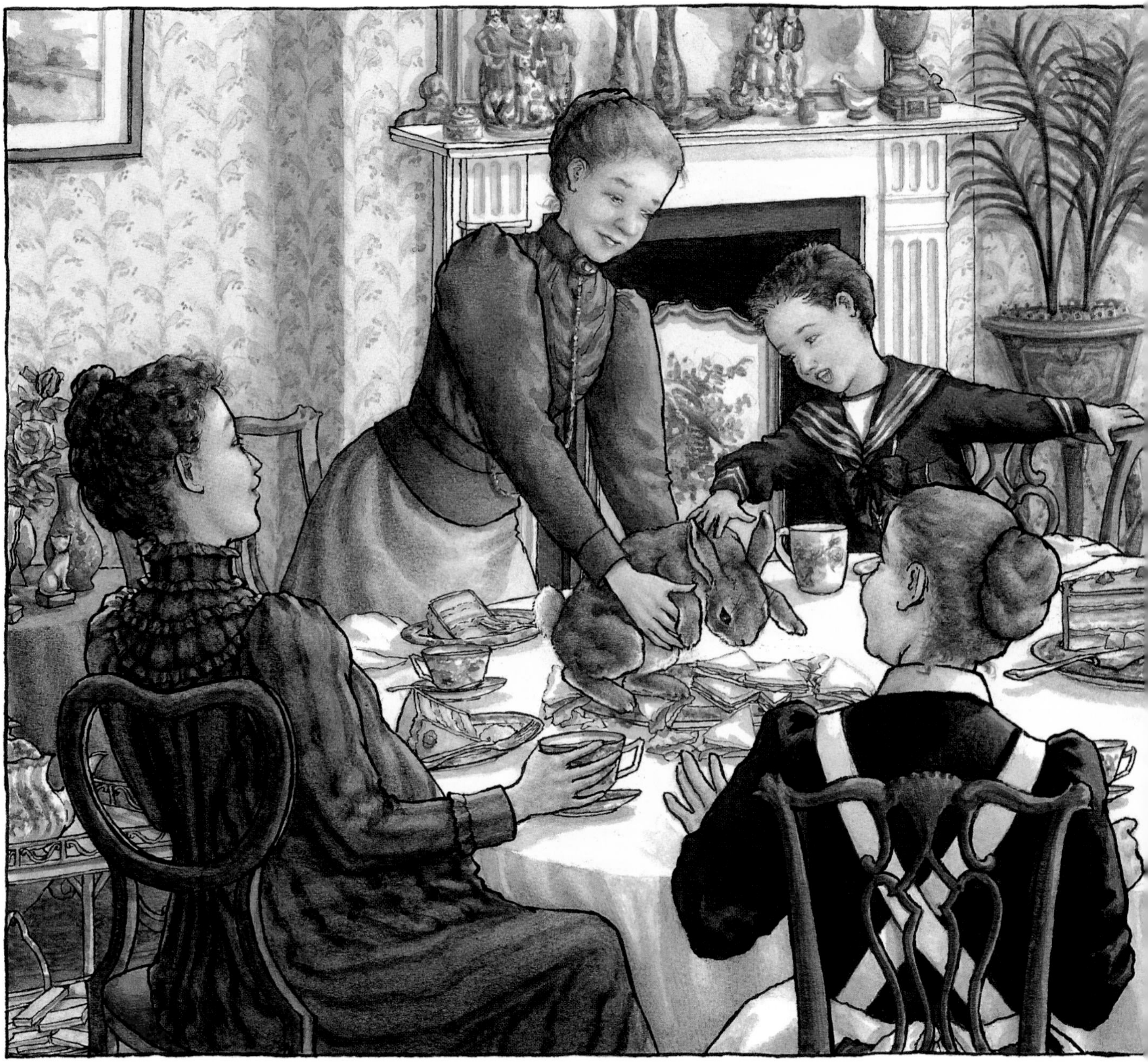

Miss Potter's rabbit, Peter, and her mice forgot the tricks she'd taught them and were naughty instead.

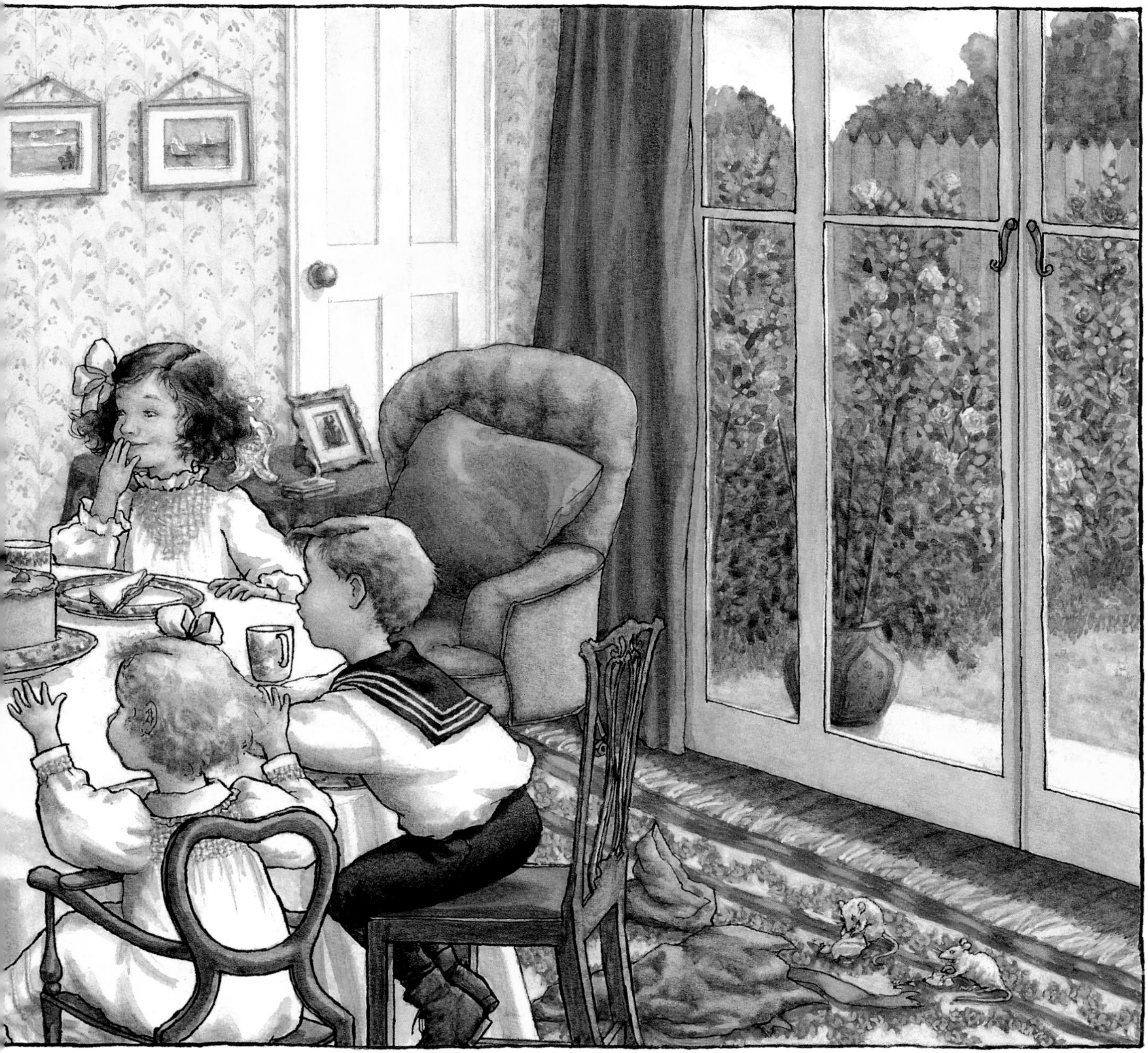

Miss Potter laughed, the children shrieked, and no one scolded.

She told jokes that made them ache with giggles.

She drew pictures and never said, "I'm tired, that's enough!"

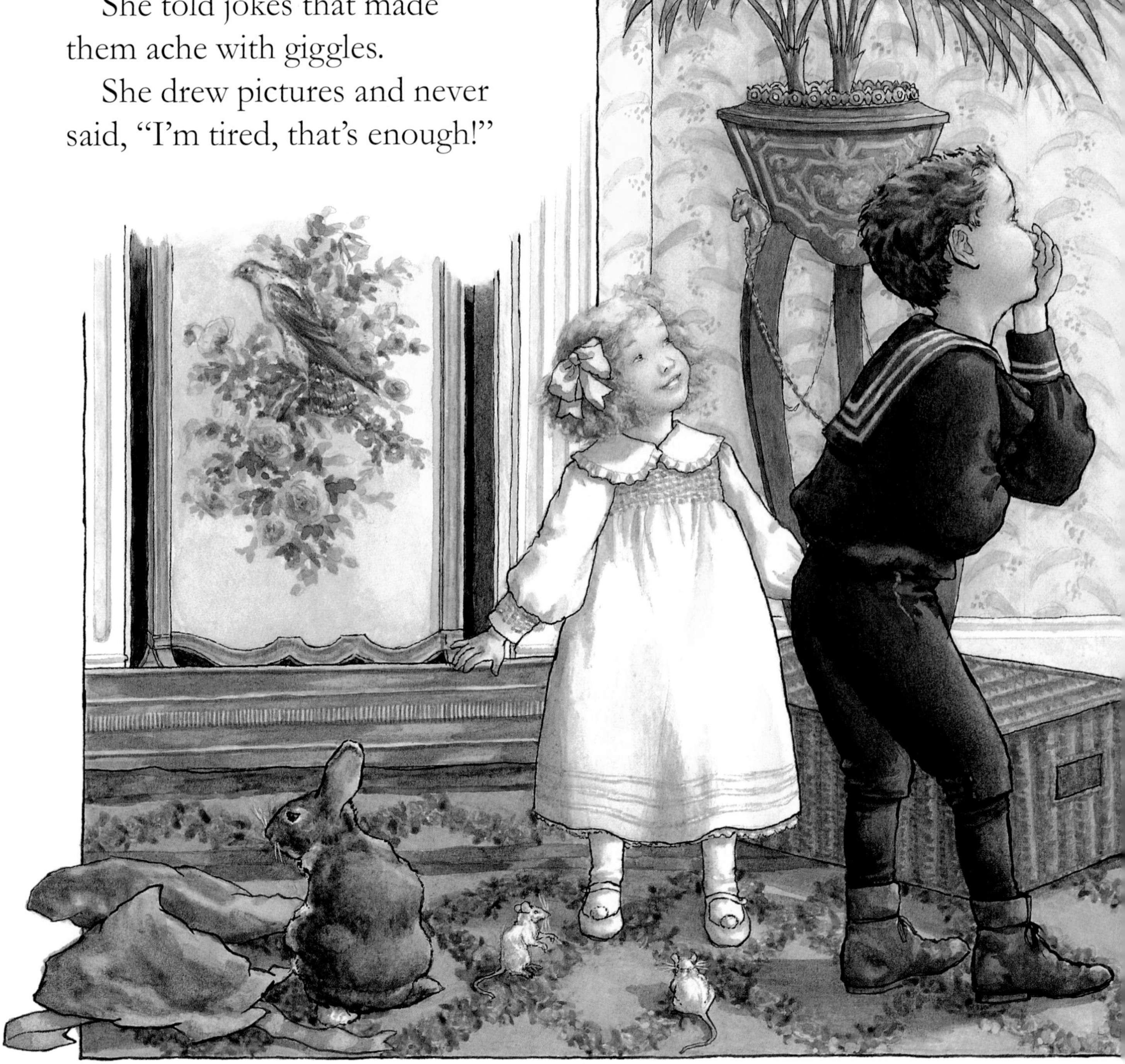

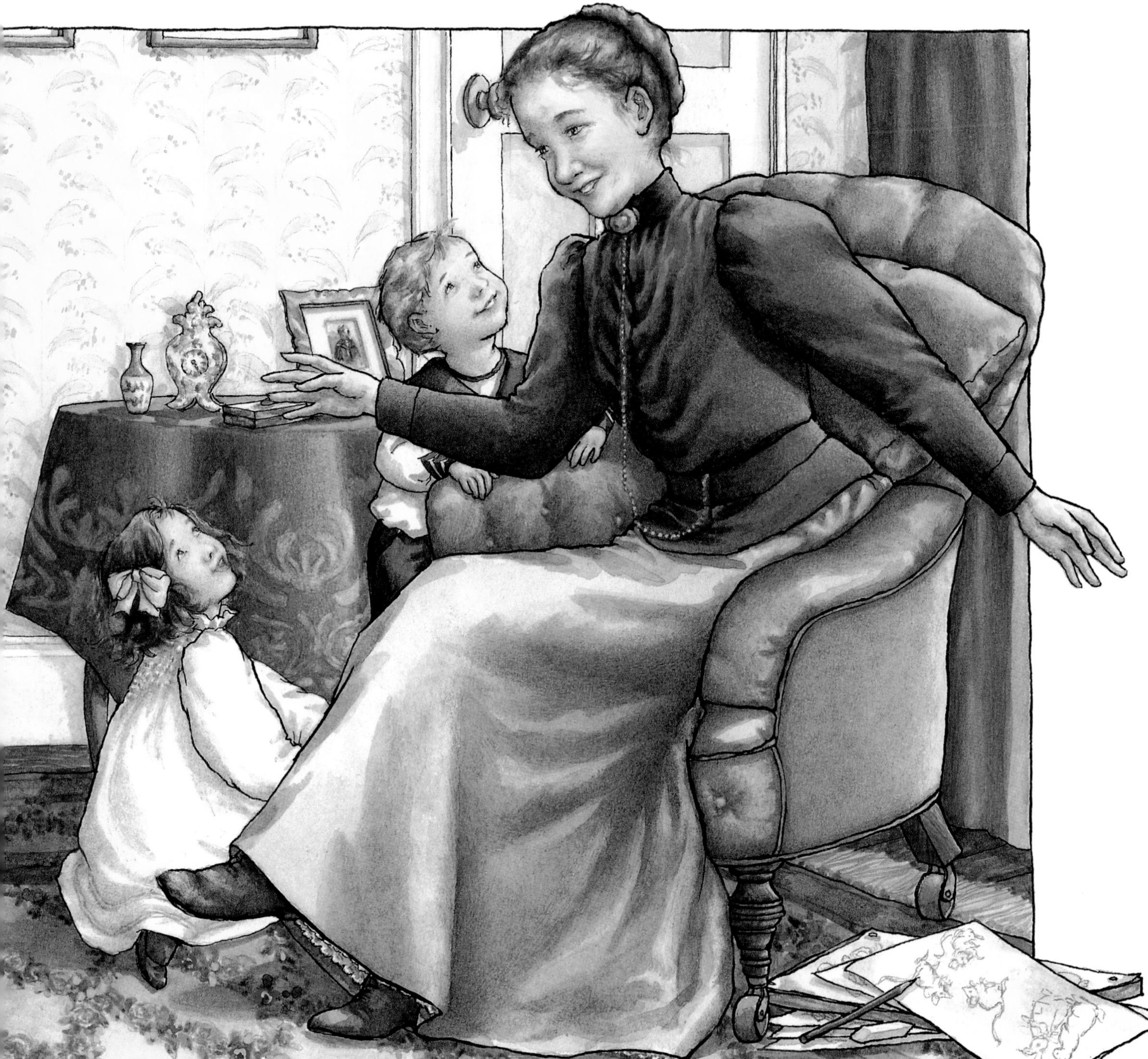

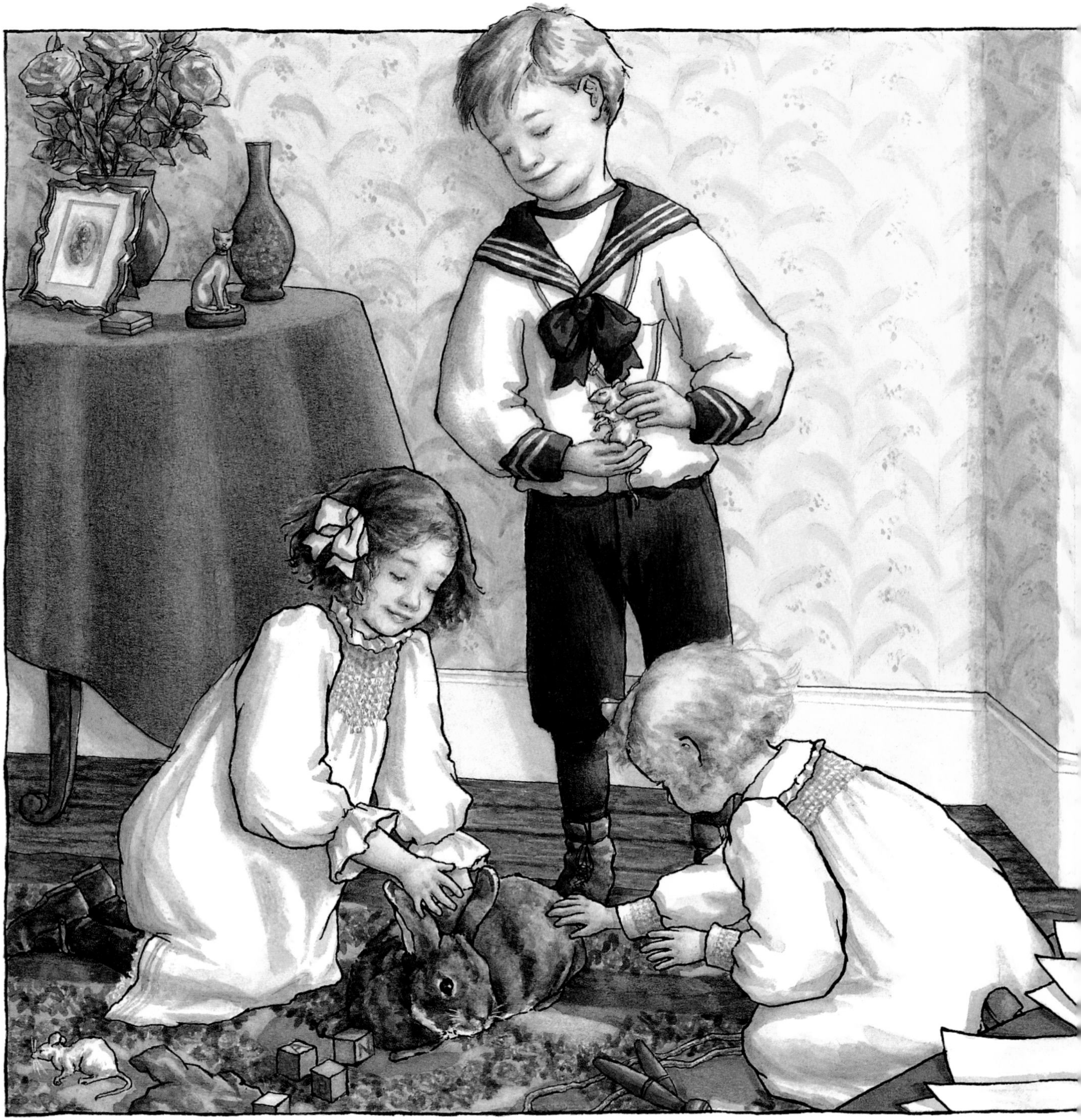

Later, when Noel had Miss Potter to himself, she whispered, "I am going to Scotland soon, so I shan't see you for a while. But I *shall* write."

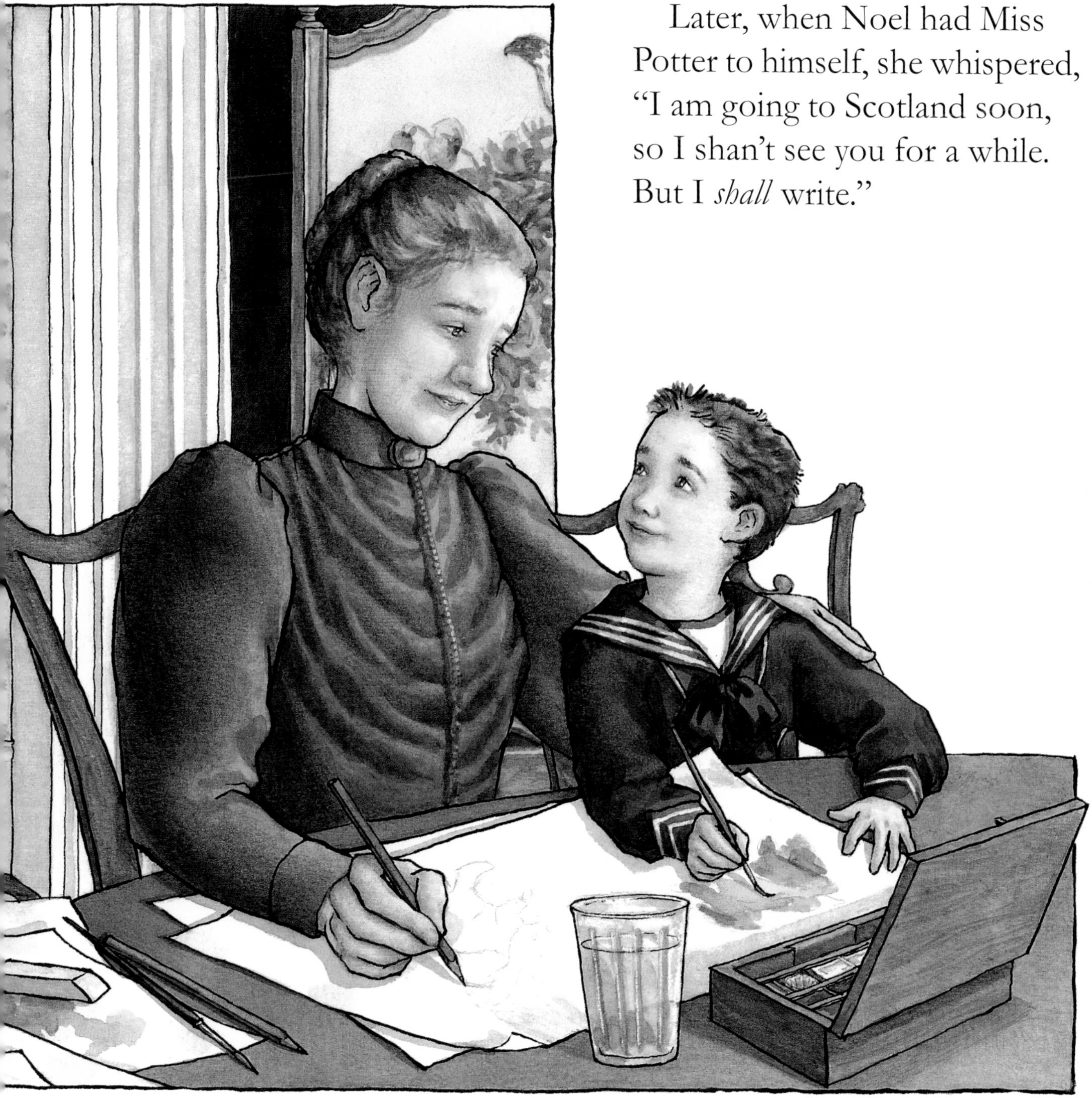

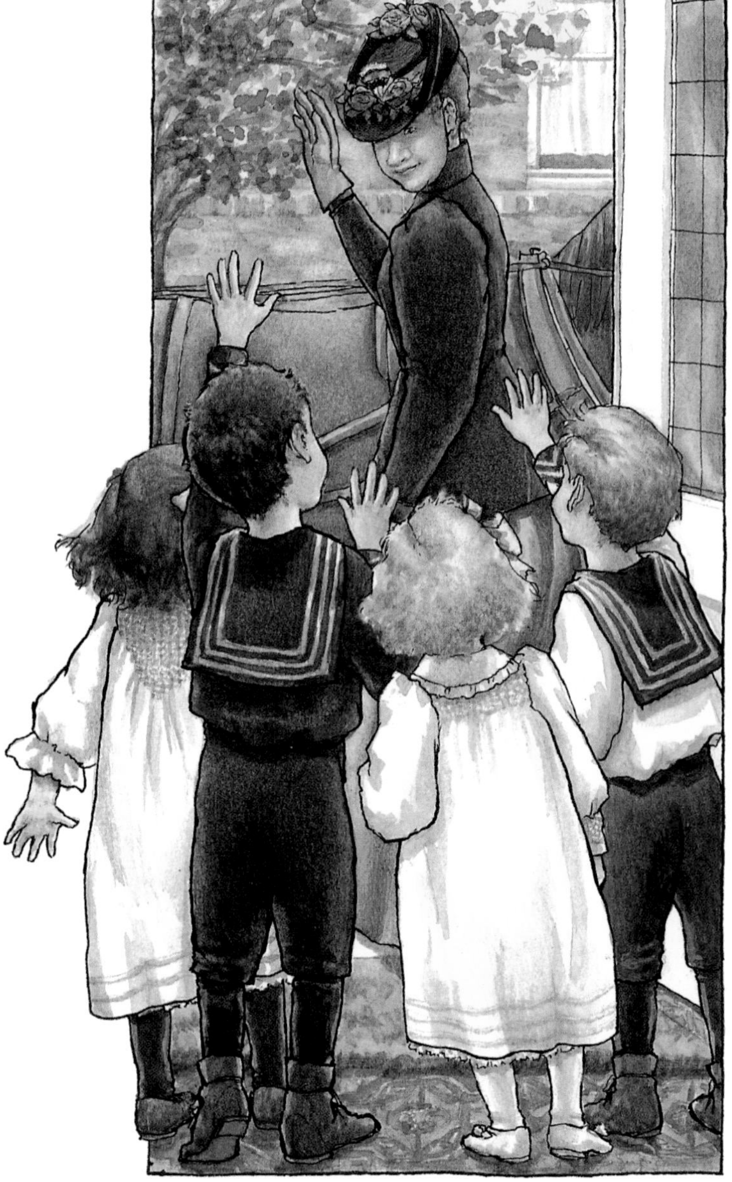

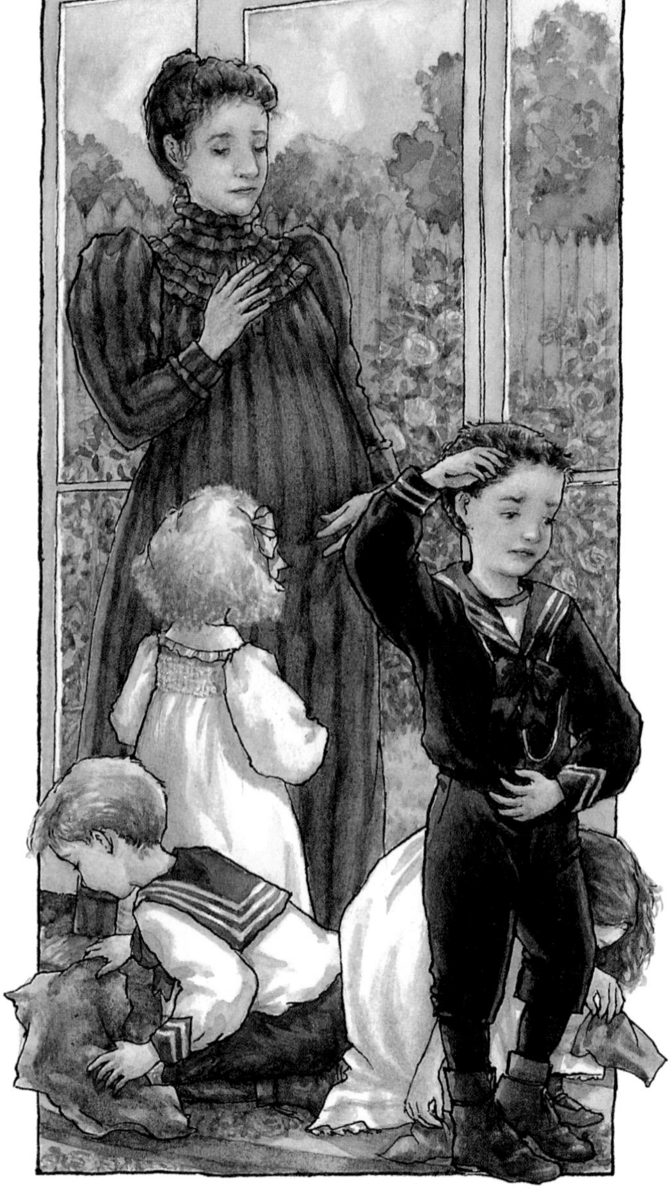

When the time came, Noel could hardly bear to see Miss Potter go. After a last good-bye, Mama said, "Now, I expect you all to tidy up."

"I'm hot, and my head hurts," grumbled Noel.

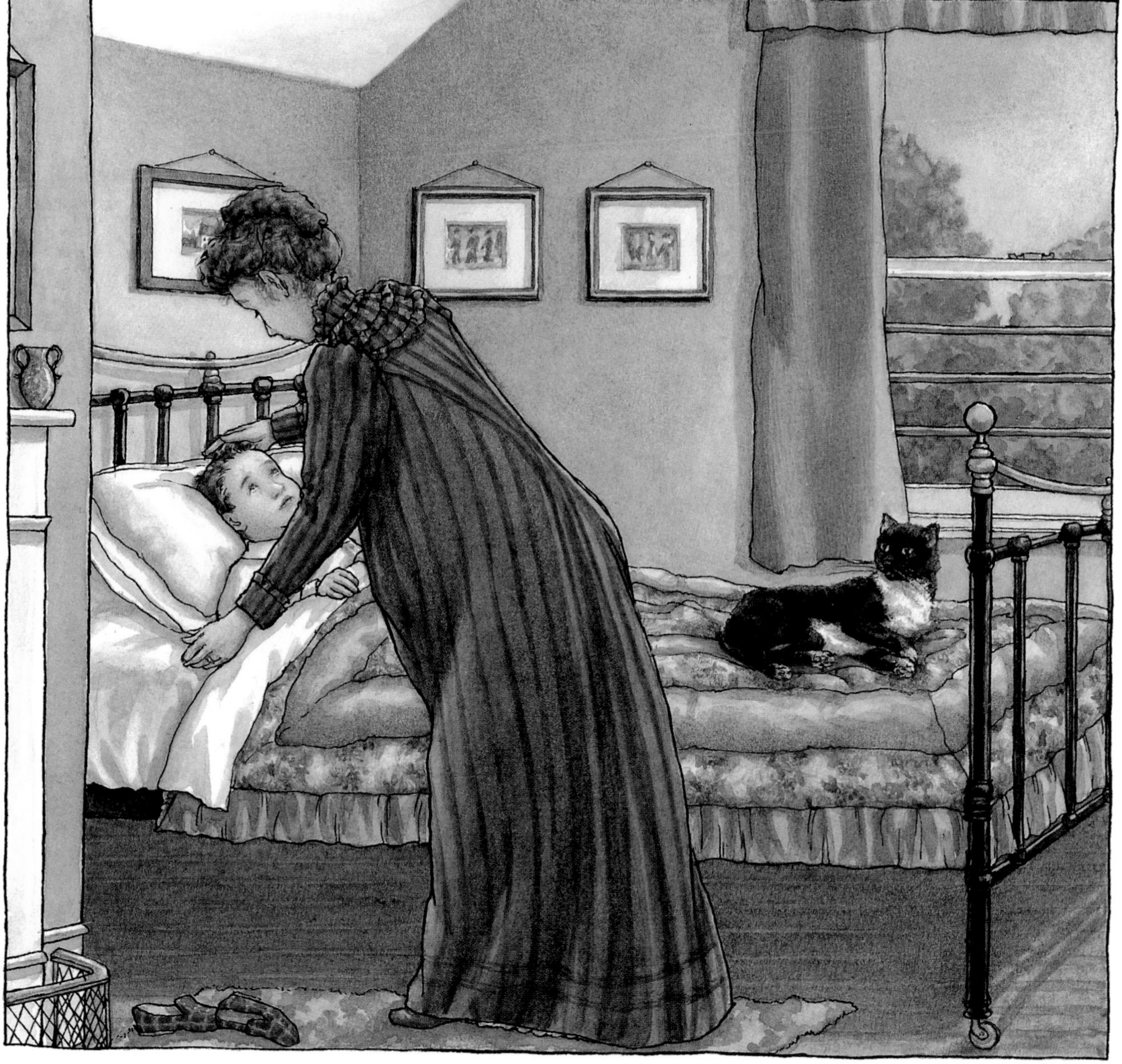

"It might just be the excitement, and too much cake," said his mother anxiously.

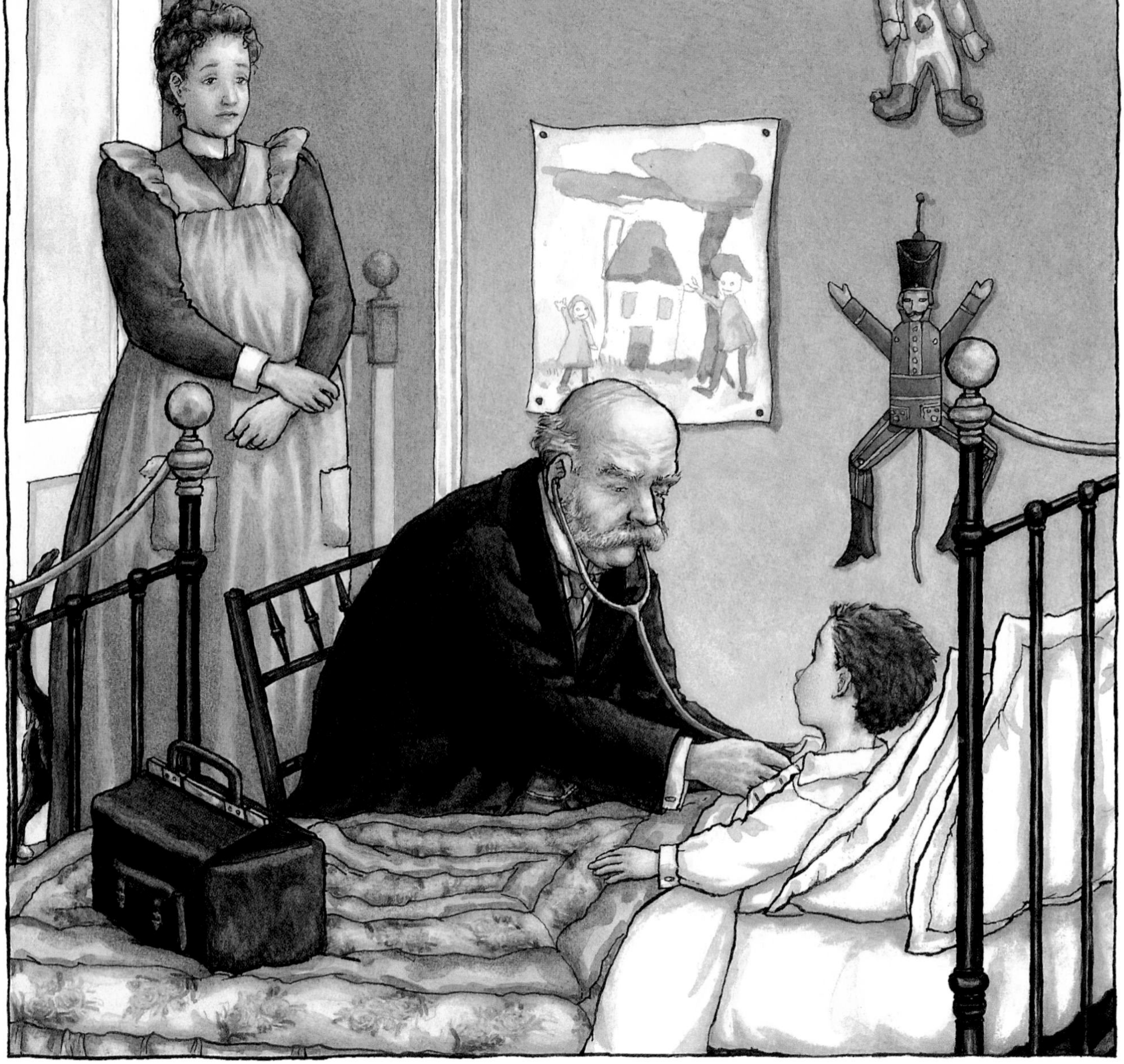

But in the morning Noel was worse, and because he was often ill, he knew he'd have to stay in bed a long, long time.

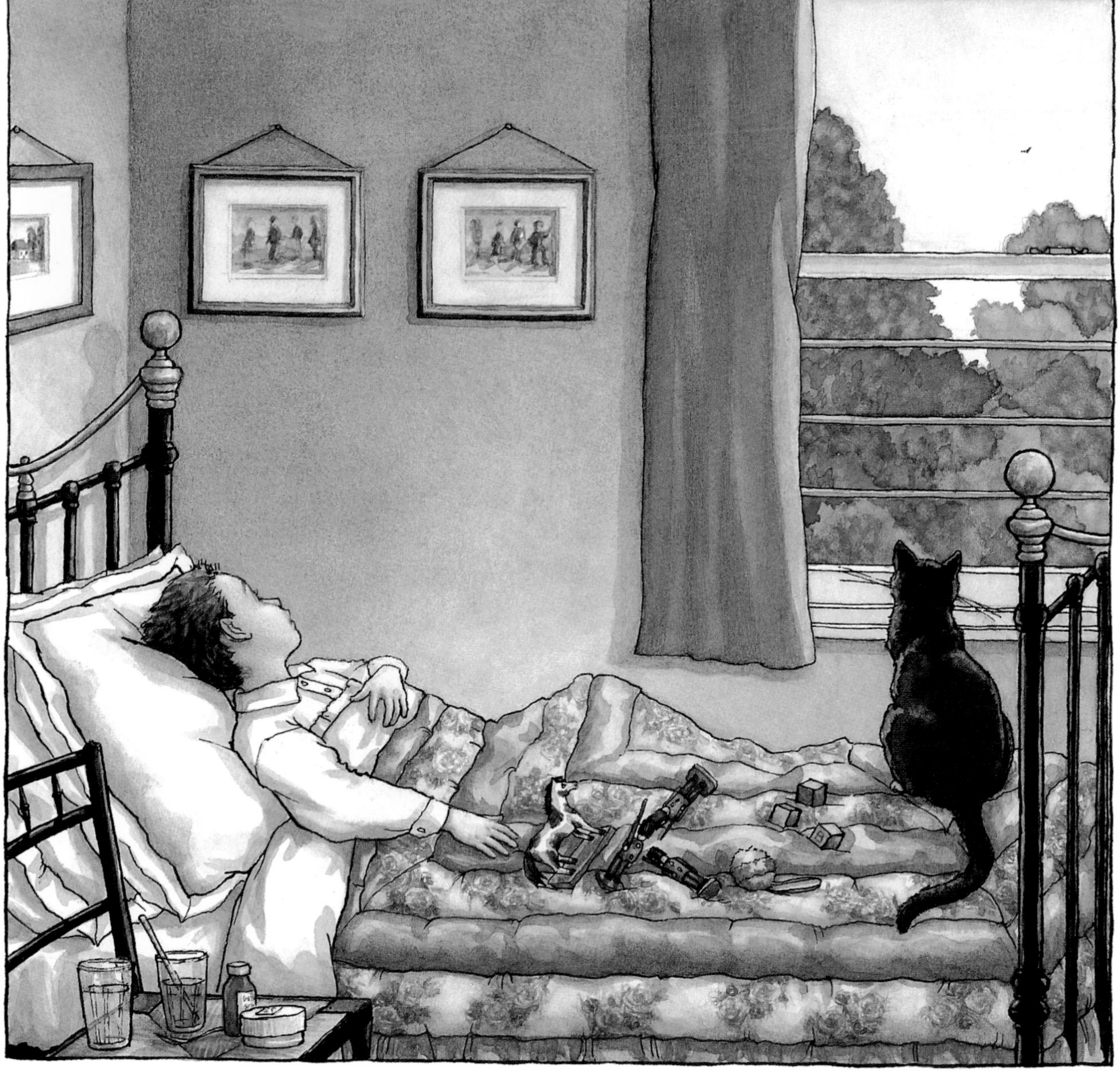

Slowly the days dragged by. Gazing out of the window, Noel listened to the sounds of breakfast, lessons, and then the shouts on the common as the others played.

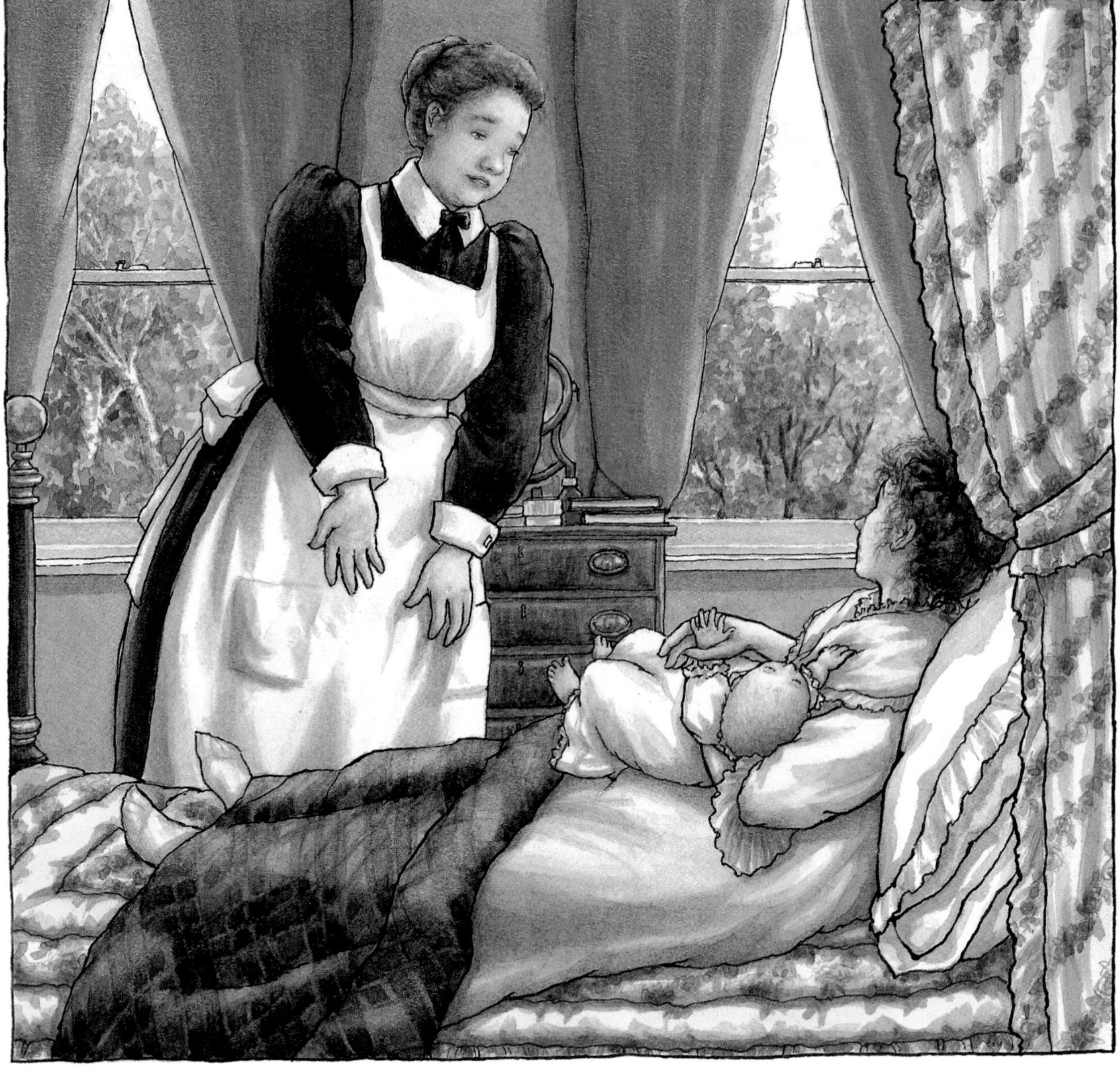

“Miss Potter would know how to cheer him, Mrs. Moore—I’m kept so busy with the younger ones,” said Nanny.

“And I’m worn to a rag with Baby,” replied Mama.

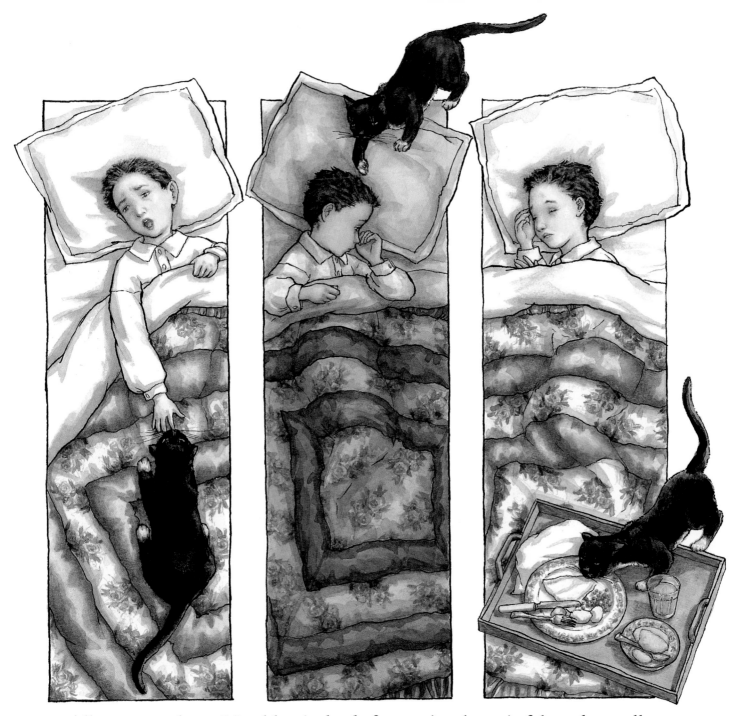

All summer long Noel lay in bed, forgetting how it felt to be well. Sometimes he cried when no one heard him call. Sometimes he slept.

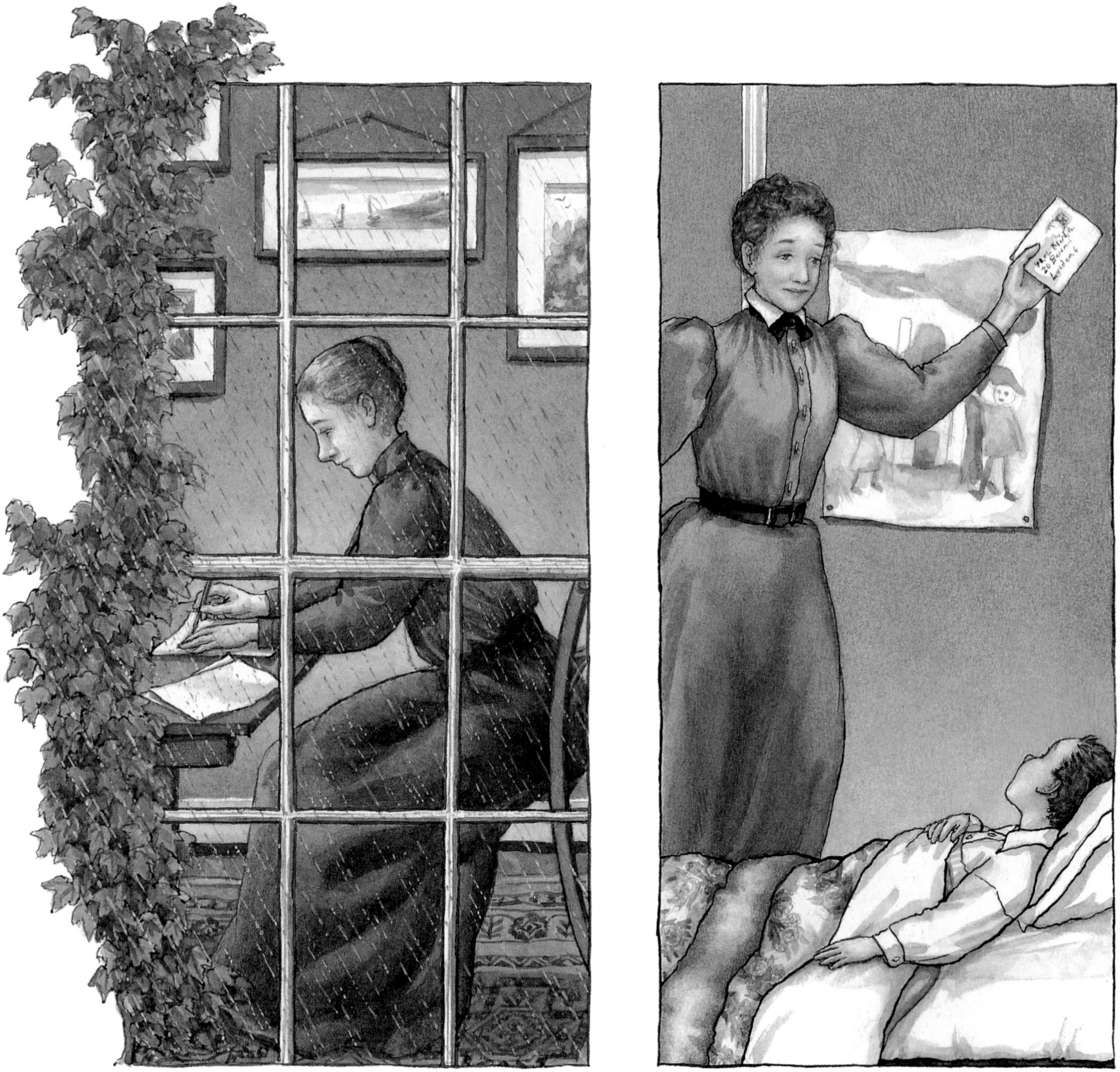

At last, with autumn in the air, a letter came for him.
"See, darling, a fat envelope, full of Miss Potter's news."

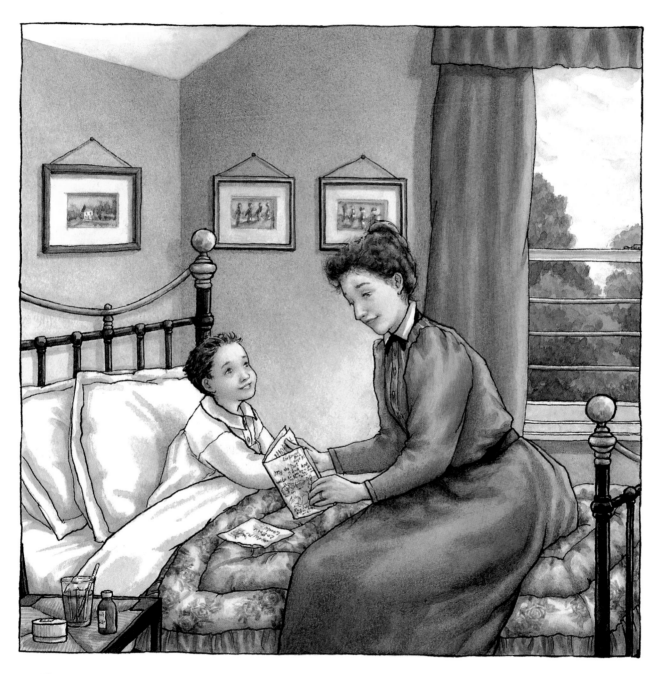

But instead of news, she had sent a *story,* with pictures. And Mama stayed, reading it over and over until she was hoarse.

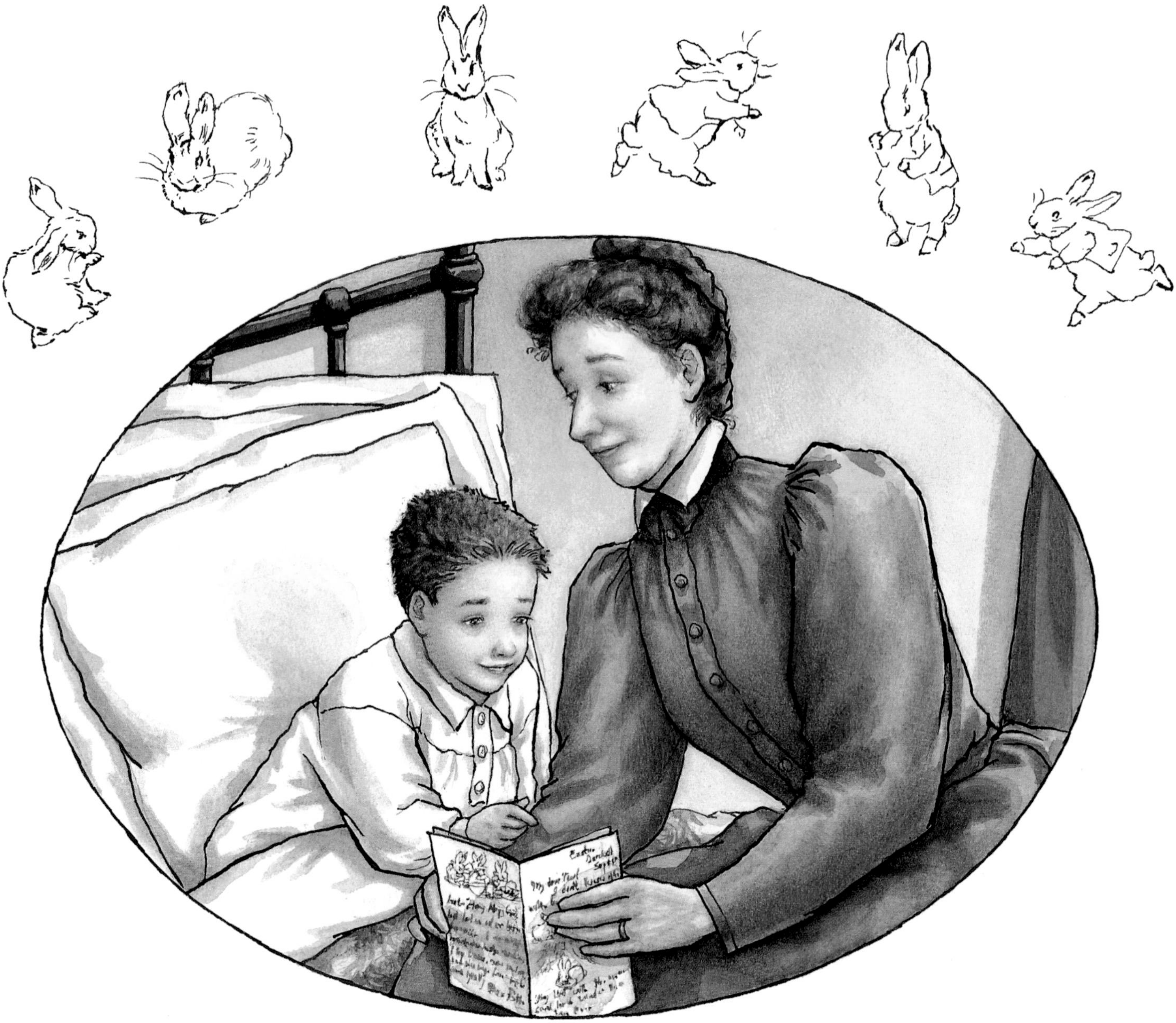

"It's about a rabbit family, but it's just like ours!" exclaimed Noel as the tale began with a mother rabbit and her children. Then, listening to the adventures of the hero, Peter Rabbit, he decided, "It's really about *me*!"

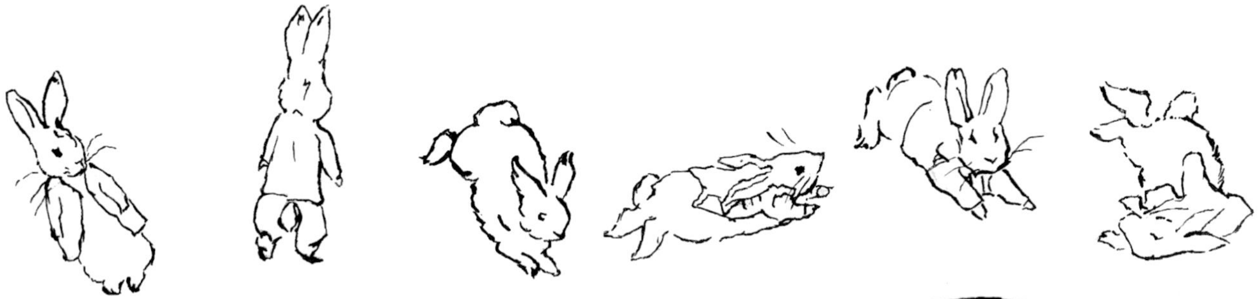

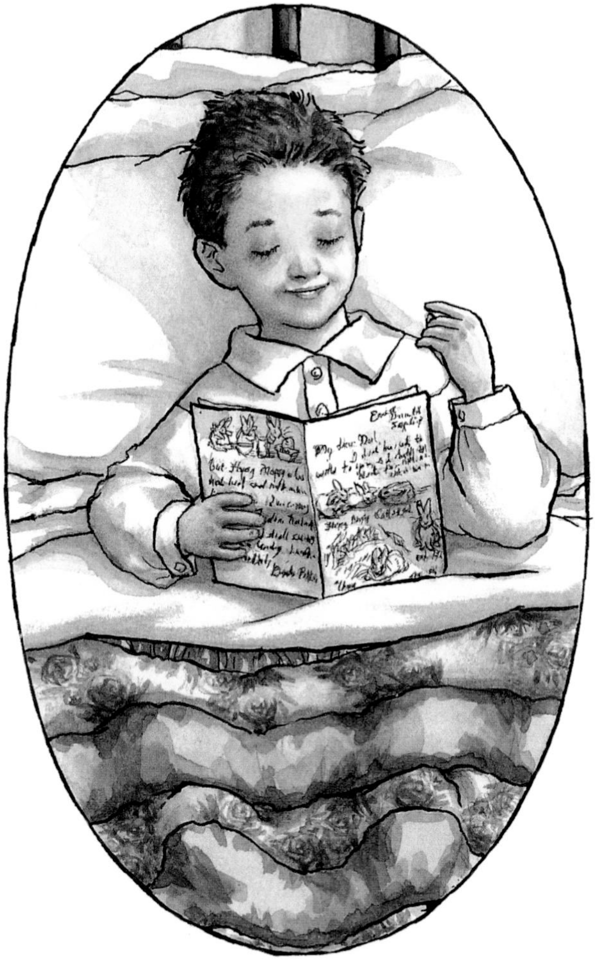

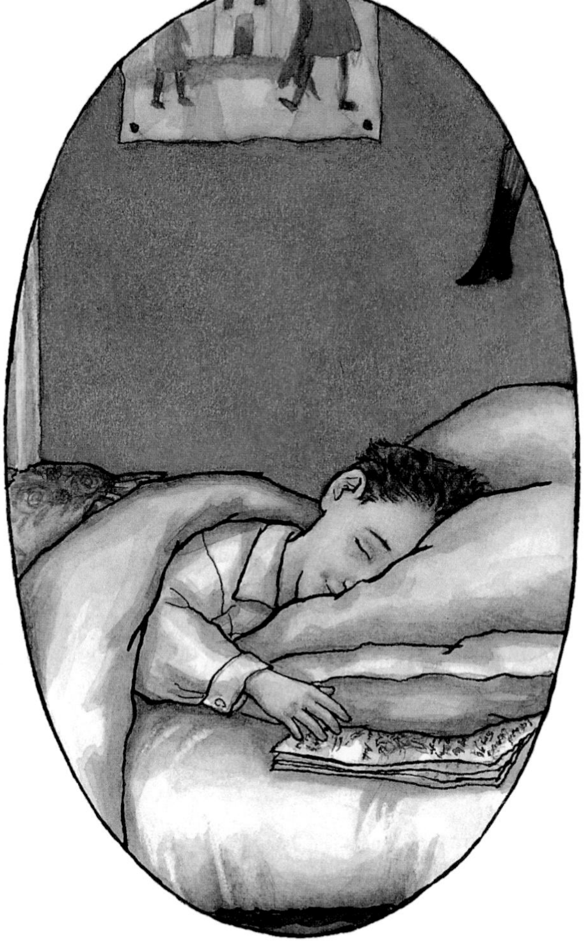

Soon Noel knew the story by heart. He read it to himself whenever he was lonely. It made him laugh. At night he dreamed that he was Peter Rabbit, and woke remembering how it felt to run. He wanted to be well.

Within a week he was getting better, and Miss Potter was back.

"You made that story up specially for me?" Noel's eyes grew dark and round as he gazed at his visitor. "Are we best friends?"

Miss Potter smiled. "Of course we are," she said gently. "Best friends."

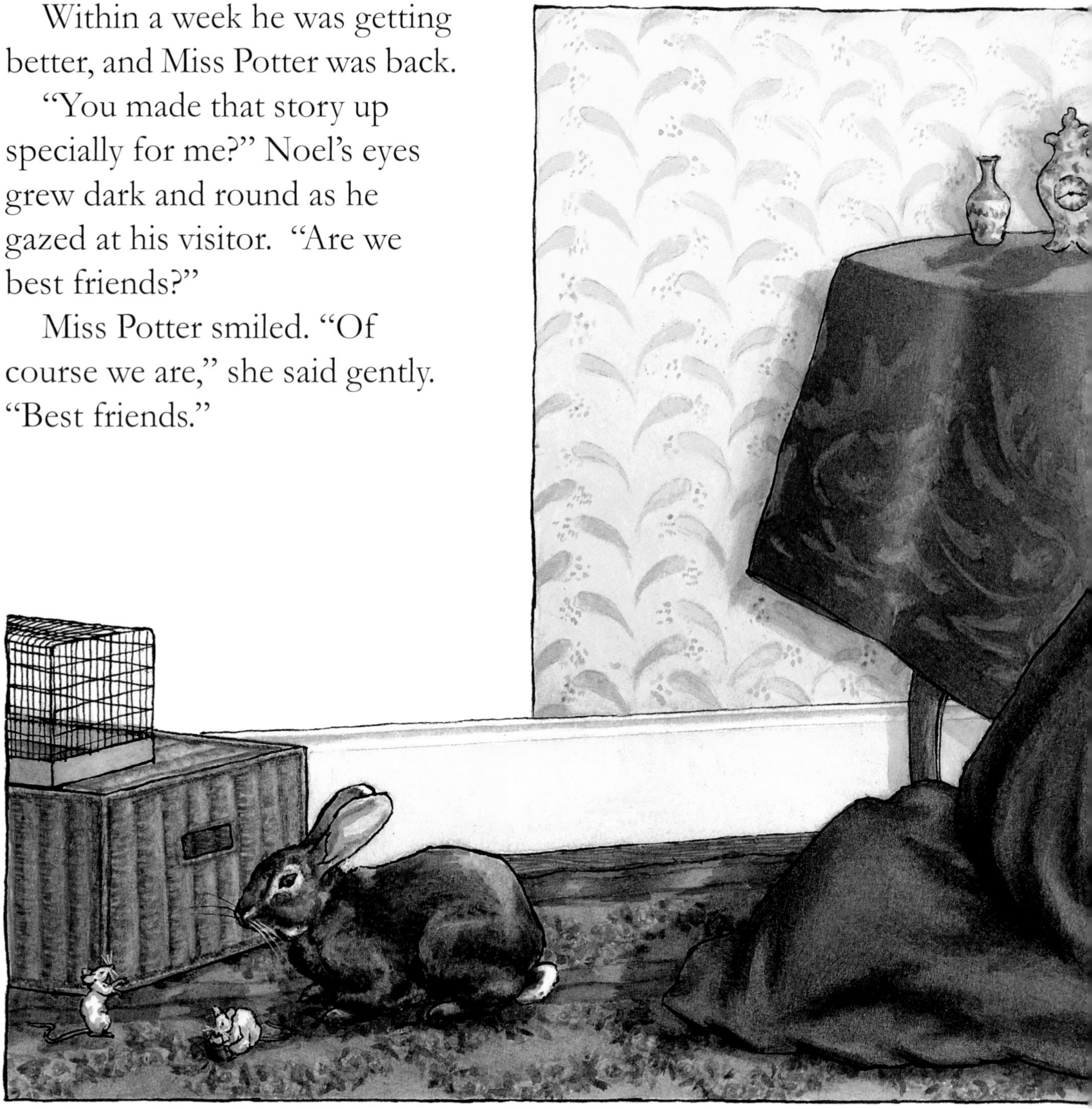

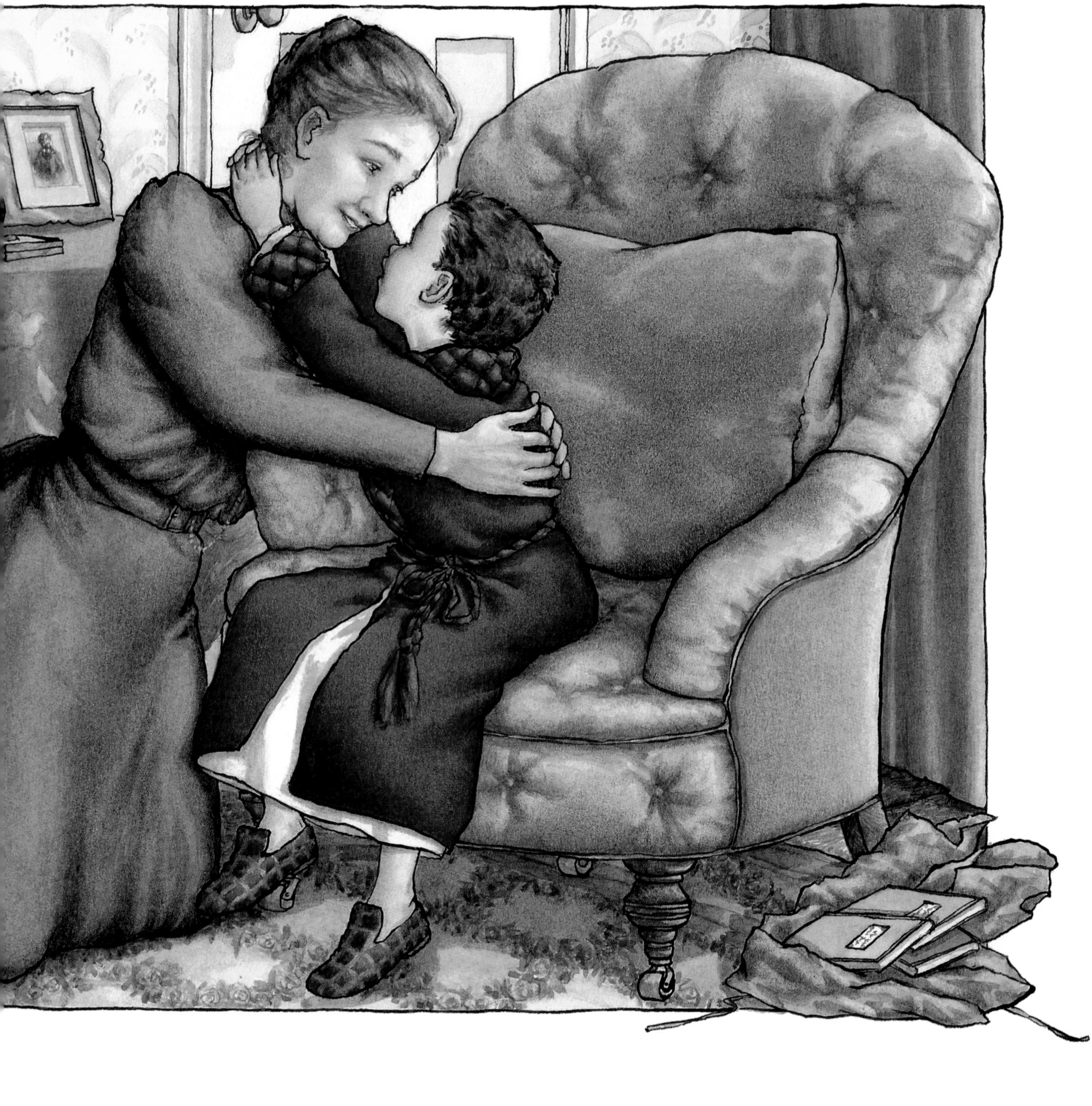

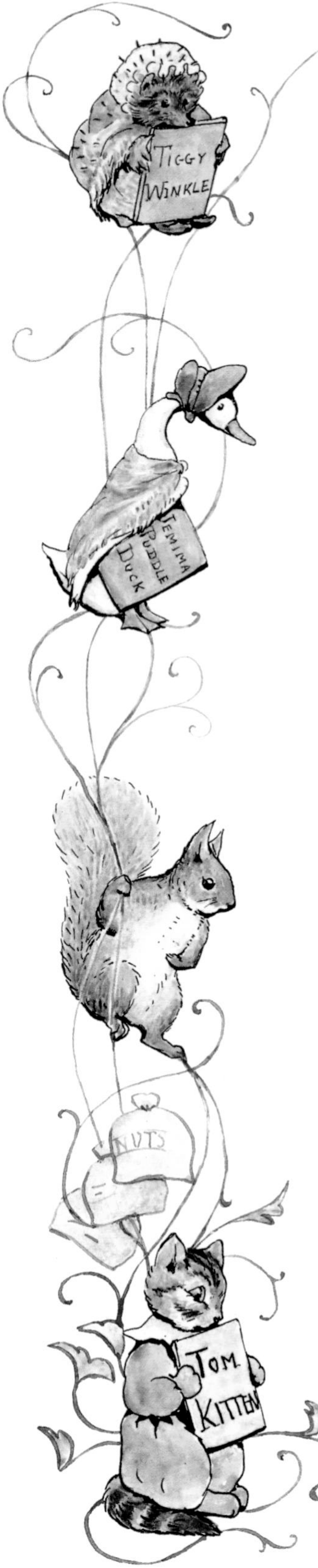
TIGGY WINKLE
JEMIMA PUDDLE DUCK
NUTS
TOM KITTEN

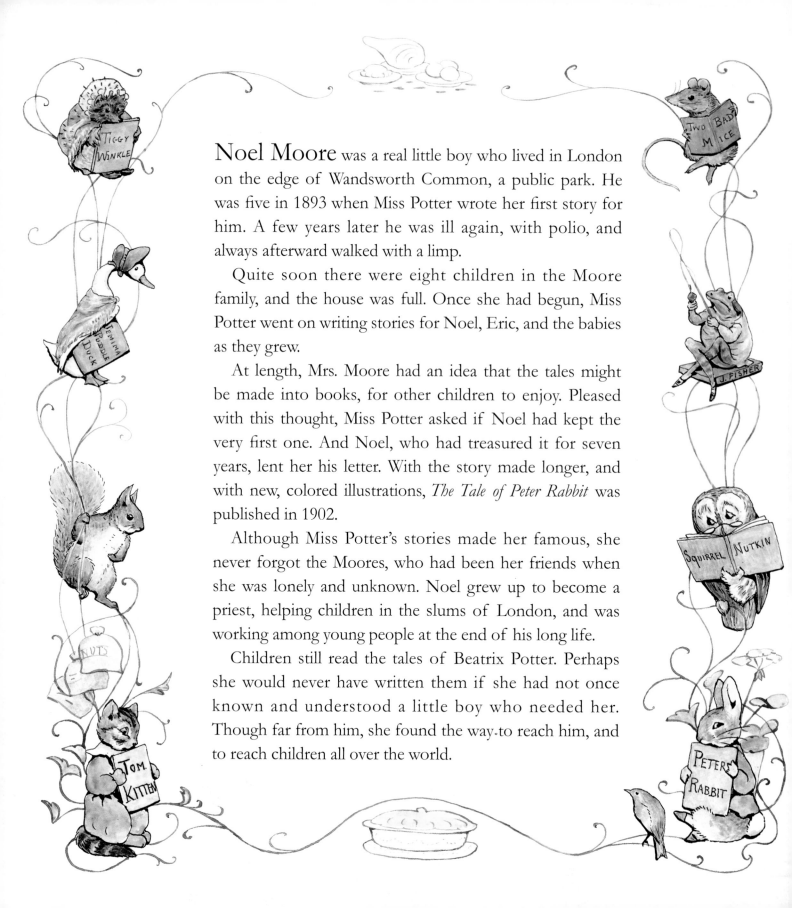

Noel Moore was a real little boy who lived in London on the edge of Wandsworth Common, a public park. He was five in 1893 when Miss Potter wrote her first story for him. A few years later he was ill again, with polio, and always afterward walked with a limp.

Quite soon there were eight children in the Moore family, and the house was full. Once she had begun, Miss Potter went on writing stories for Noel, Eric, and the babies as they grew.

At length, Mrs. Moore had an idea that the tales might be made into books, for other children to enjoy. Pleased with this thought, Miss Potter asked if Noel had kept the very first one. And Noel, who had treasured it for seven years, lent her his letter. With the story made longer, and with new, colored illustrations, *The Tale of Peter Rabbit* was published in 1902.

Although Miss Potter's stories made her famous, she never forgot the Moores, who had been her friends when she was lonely and unknown. Noel grew up to become a priest, helping children in the slums of London, and was working among young people at the end of his long life.

Children still read the tales of Beatrix Potter. Perhaps she would never have written them if she had not once known and understood a little boy who needed her. Though far from him, she found the way to reach him, and to reach children all over the world.

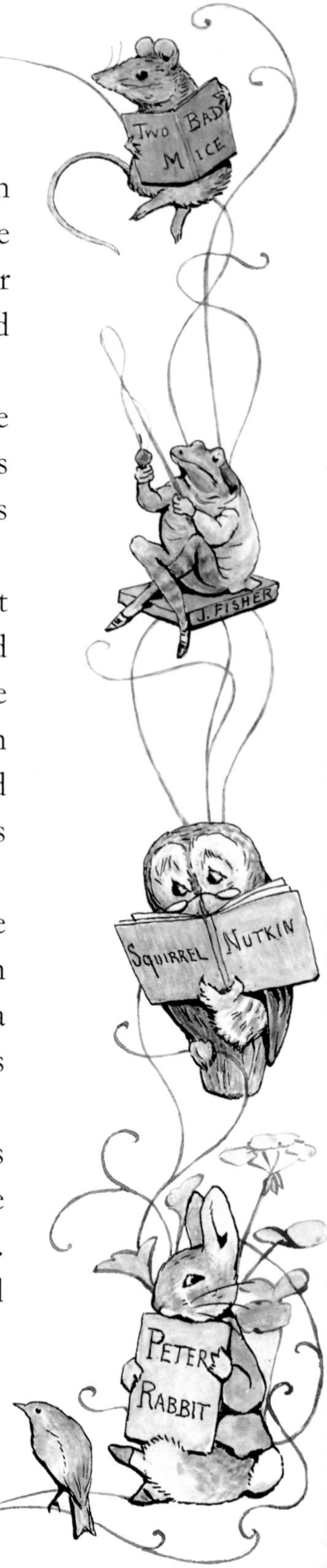
TWO BAD MICE
J. FISHER
SQUIRREL NUTKIN
PETER RABBIT

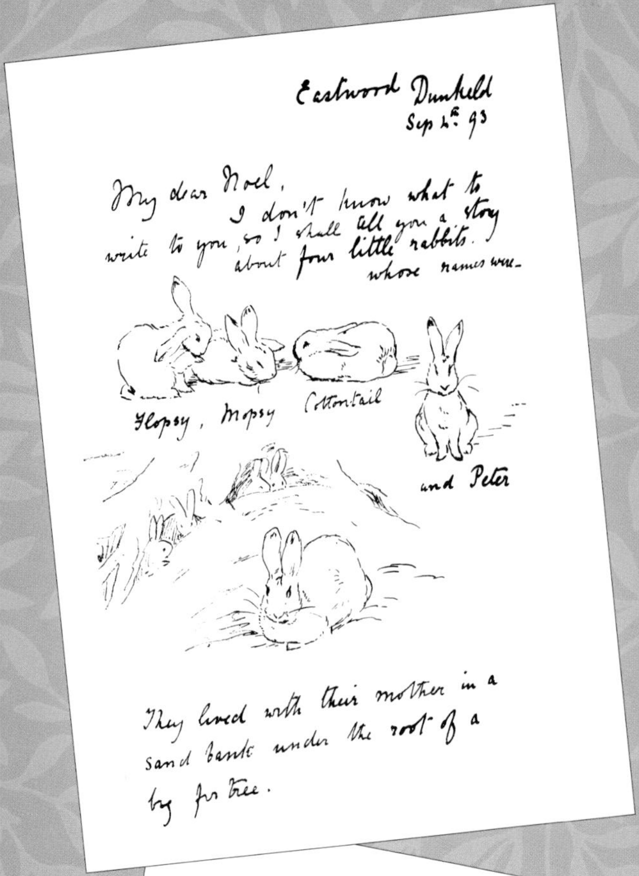

Eastwood Dunkeld
Sep 4th 93

My dear Noel,
I don't know what to write to you, so I shall tell you a story about four little rabbits whose names were—

Flopsy, Mopsy, Cottontail and Peter

They lived with their mother in a sand bank under the root of a big fir tree.

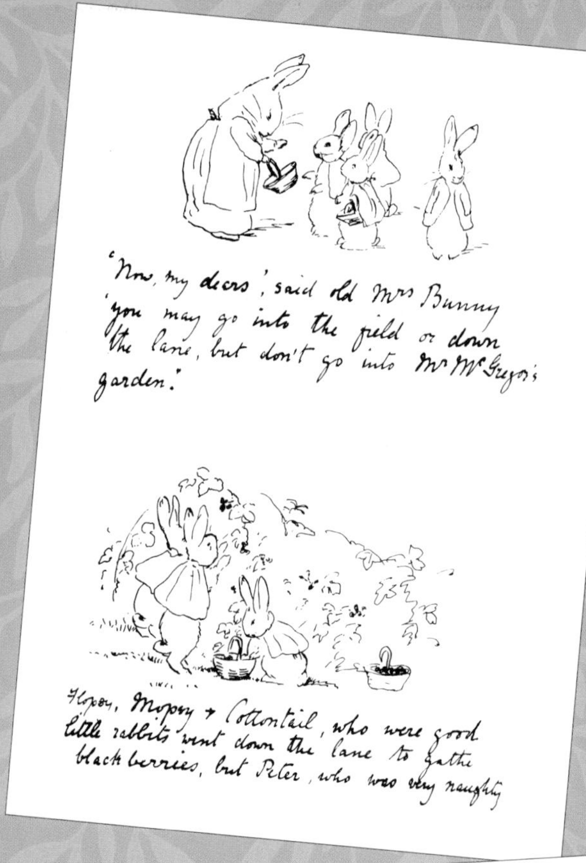

'Now, my dears', said old Mrs Bunny 'you may go into the field or down the lane, but don't go into Mr McGregor's garden.'

Flopsy, Mopsy & Cottontail, who were good little rabbits went down the lane to gather blackberries, but Peter, who was very naughty

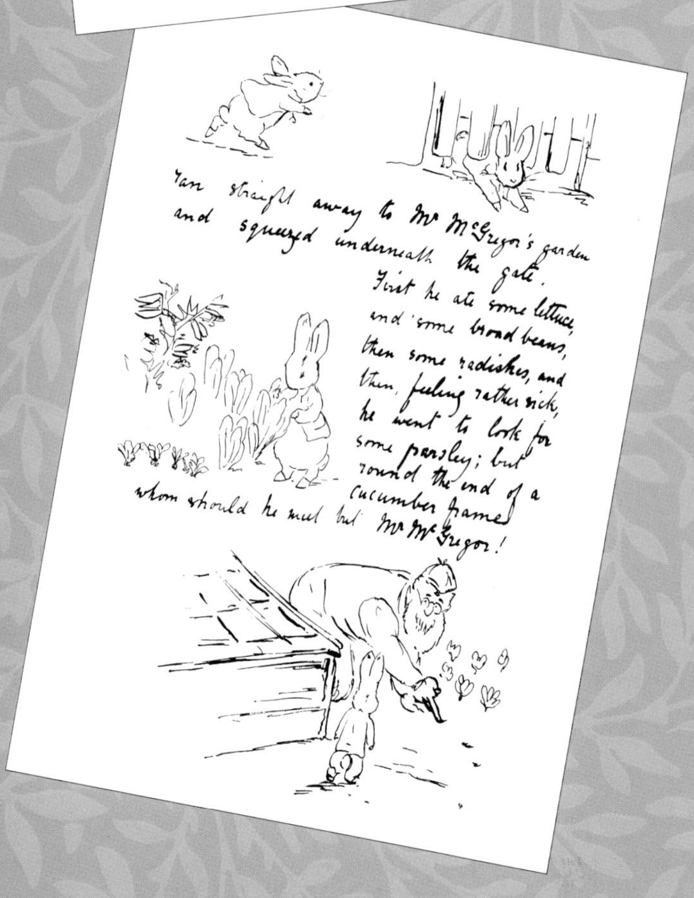

ran straight away to Mr McGregor's garden and squeezed underneath the gate.
First he ate some lettuce, and some broad beans, then some radishes, and then, feeling rather sick, he went to look for some parsley; but round the end of a cucumber frame whom should he meet but Mr McGregor!

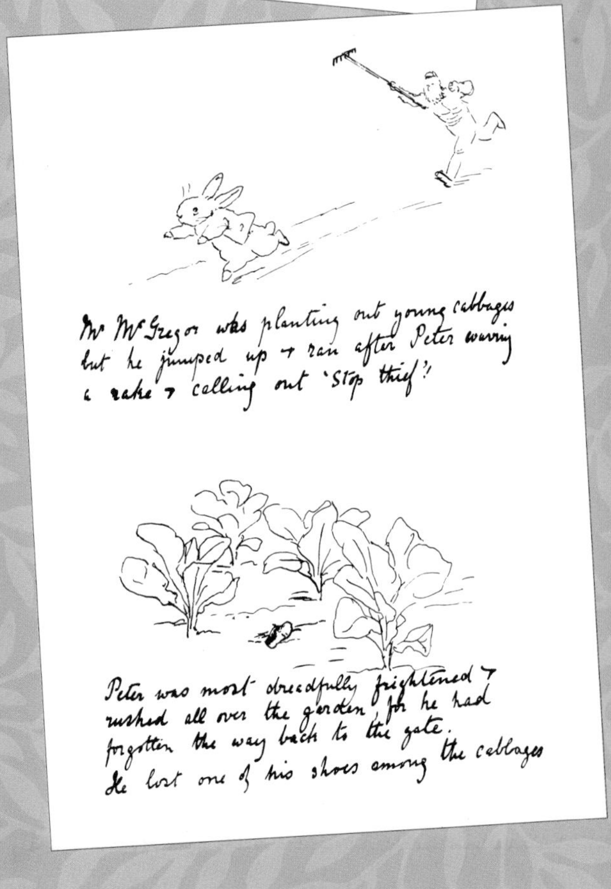

Mr McGregor was planting out young cabbages but he jumped up & ran after Peter waving a rake & calling out 'Stop thief'!

Peter was most dreadfully frightened & rushed all over the garden for he had forgotten the way back to the gate. He lost one of his shoes among the cabbages

All About Your
Lungs

Donna Bailey

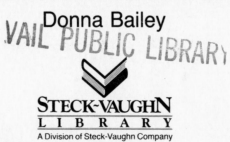

STECK-VAUGHN
LIBRARY
A Division of Steck-Vaughn Company

Austin, Texas

How to Use This Book

This book tells you many things about your lungs and how you breathe. There is a Table of Contents on the next page. It shows you what each double page of the book is about. For example, pages 12 and 13 tell you "Why We Breathe."

On many of these pages you will find some words that are printed in **bold** type. The bold type shows you that these words are in the Glossary on pages 46 and 47. The Glossary explains the meaning of some words that may be new to you.

At the very end of the book there is an Index. The Index tells you where to find certain words in the book. For example, you can use it to look up words like alveoli, respiratory system, vocal cords, and many other words to do with your lungs and breathing.

Printed and bound in the United States of America
1 2 3 4 5 6 7 8 9 0 LB 95 94 93 92 91

Library of Congress Cataloging-In-Publication Data

Bailey, Donna.
All about your lungs / Donna Bailey.
p. cm. — (Health facts)
Summary: Describes the organs of the respiratory system and their functions and discusses the consequences of disease and prolonged abuse on this vital system.
Includes index.
ISBN 0-8114-2782-X
1. Lungs—Juvenile literature. 2. Respiration—Juvenile literature. [1. Respiratory system.] I. Title. II. Series: Bailey, Donna. Health facts.
QP121.B18 1990
612.2—dc20 90-41009
CIP AC

Contents

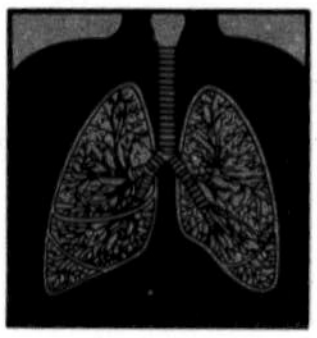

Introduction

All living things need **oxygen** in order to stay alive.

Each kind of living creature gets oxygen in its own way. Fish and crabs breathe in oxygen from the water through their **gills.** Birds and **mammals** breathe in oxygen from the air into their **lungs.**

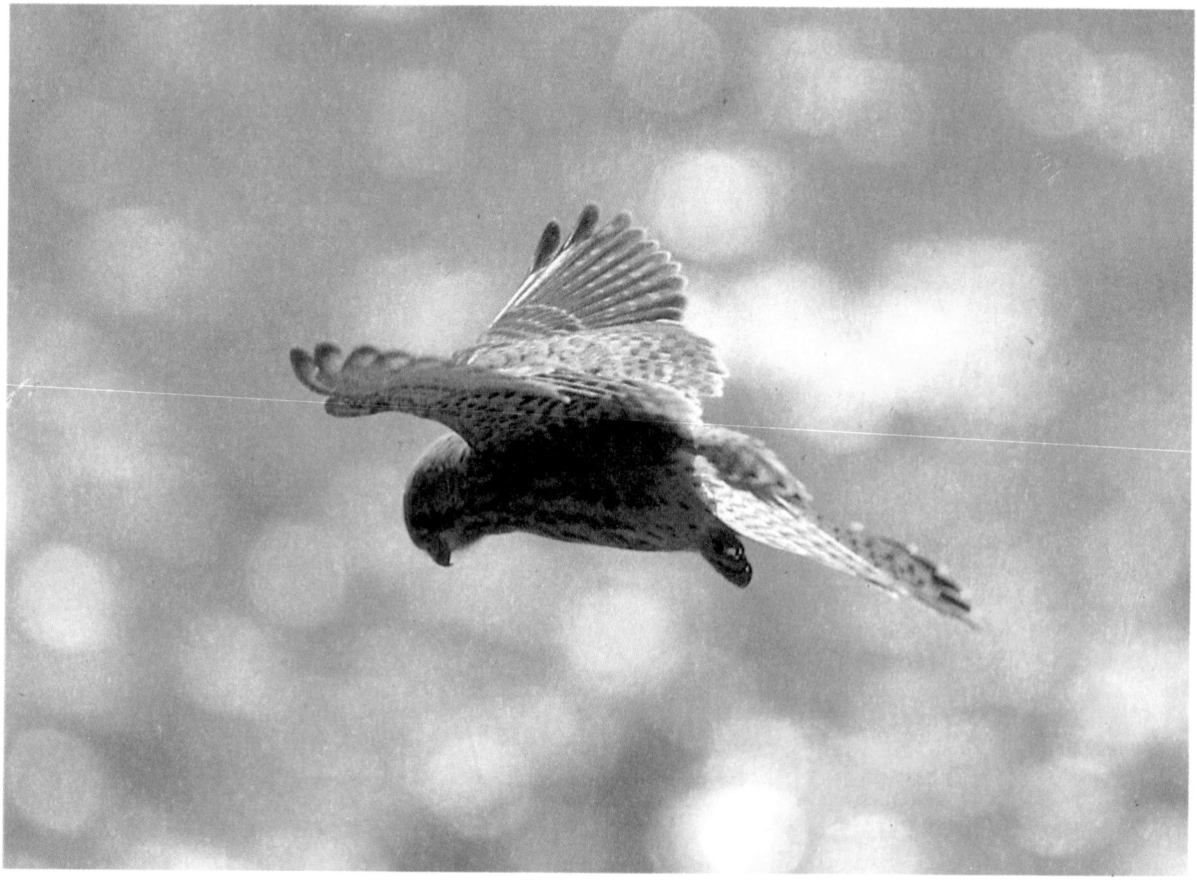

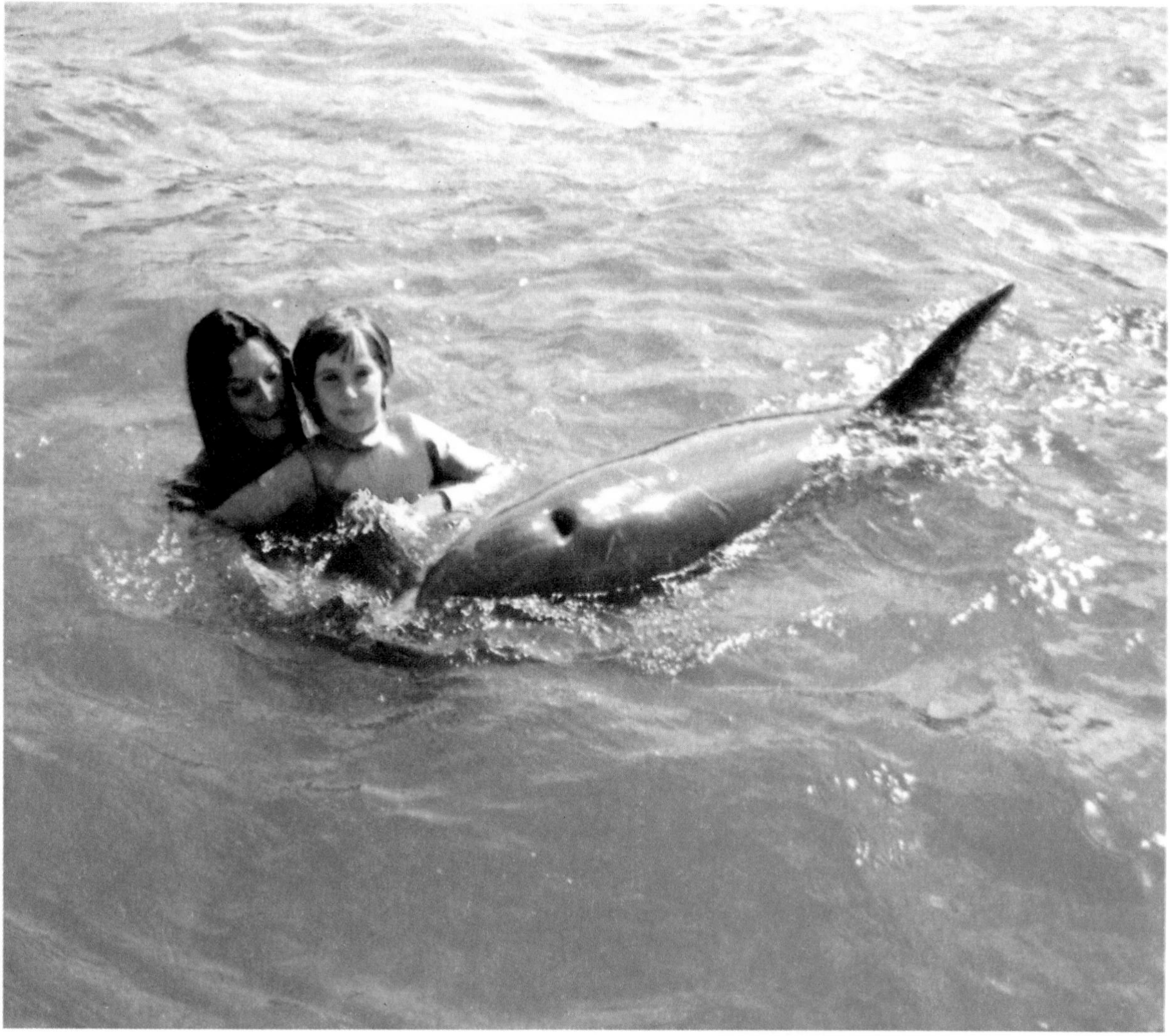

The dolphin in the picture is not a fish but a mammal with lungs, like us. It swims up to the surface to breathe in air, and it breathes out through the blow-hole on its head.

Birds need a lot of oxygen to fly. The movement of their wings helps to force air in and out of their lungs.

Long Ago

This painting by Michelangelo shows his idea of God creating the first man, Adam. Long ago, people knew that air was important to stay alive, but they did not know why. They thought that only the gods could breathe life into a living creature.

The ancient Greeks tried to understand why air is important to the body. One Greek thinker taught that everything was made out of four **elements:** earth, air, fire, and water.

Another Greek teacher, Aristotle, taught that a special kind of heat inside the body keeps us alive. He thought this heat came from the heart, and the air we breathe kept the fire burning and cooled our bodies.

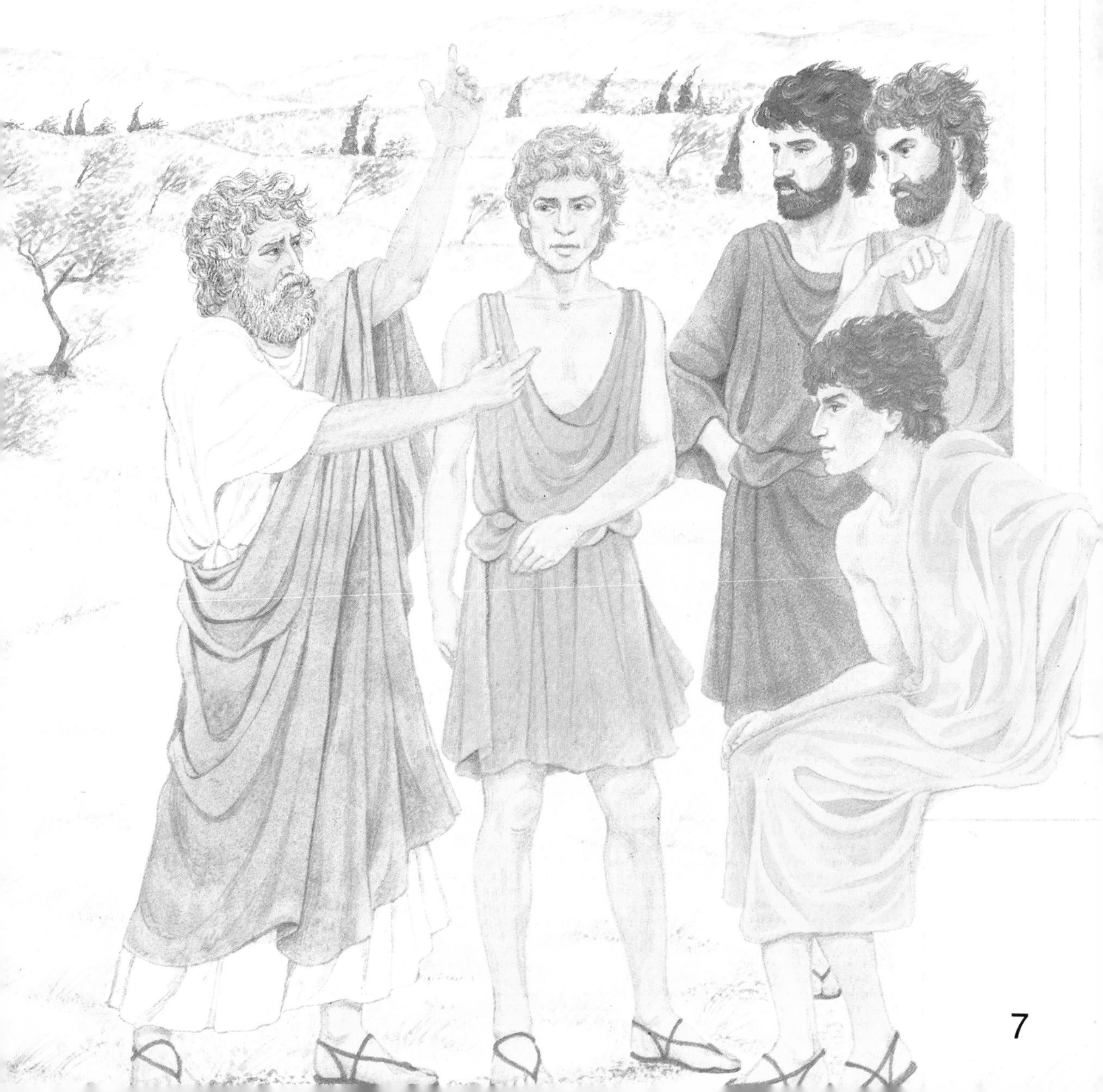

Finding Out

In the 1600s, people began to understand more about air. The picture shows an air pump that was used to raise water through underground pipes by **pressure.**

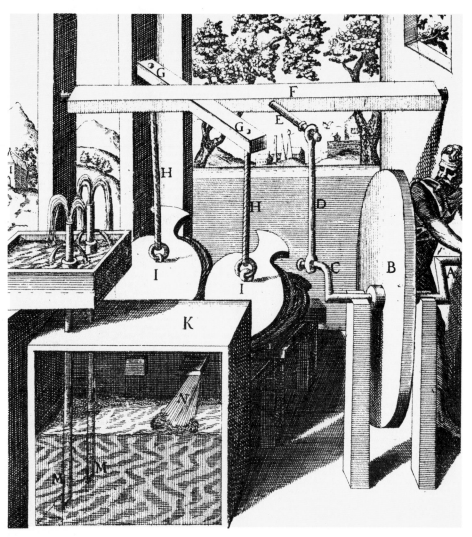

Scientists began to study how the body works. The scientist Robert Hooke found that parts of our bodies act like pumps.

The picture below, painted in 1768, shows a scientist trying out an air pump. Without air, the bird in the bowl soon died. People wondered what was in the air that kept the bird alive.

This picture shows Antoine Lavoiser, who was the first person to discover that oxygen is one of the gases found in air.

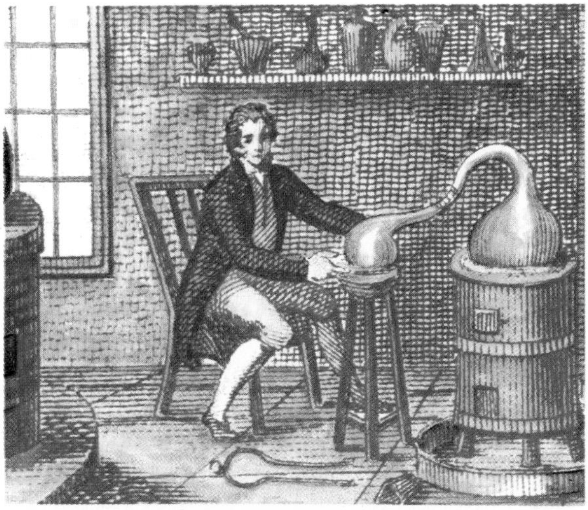

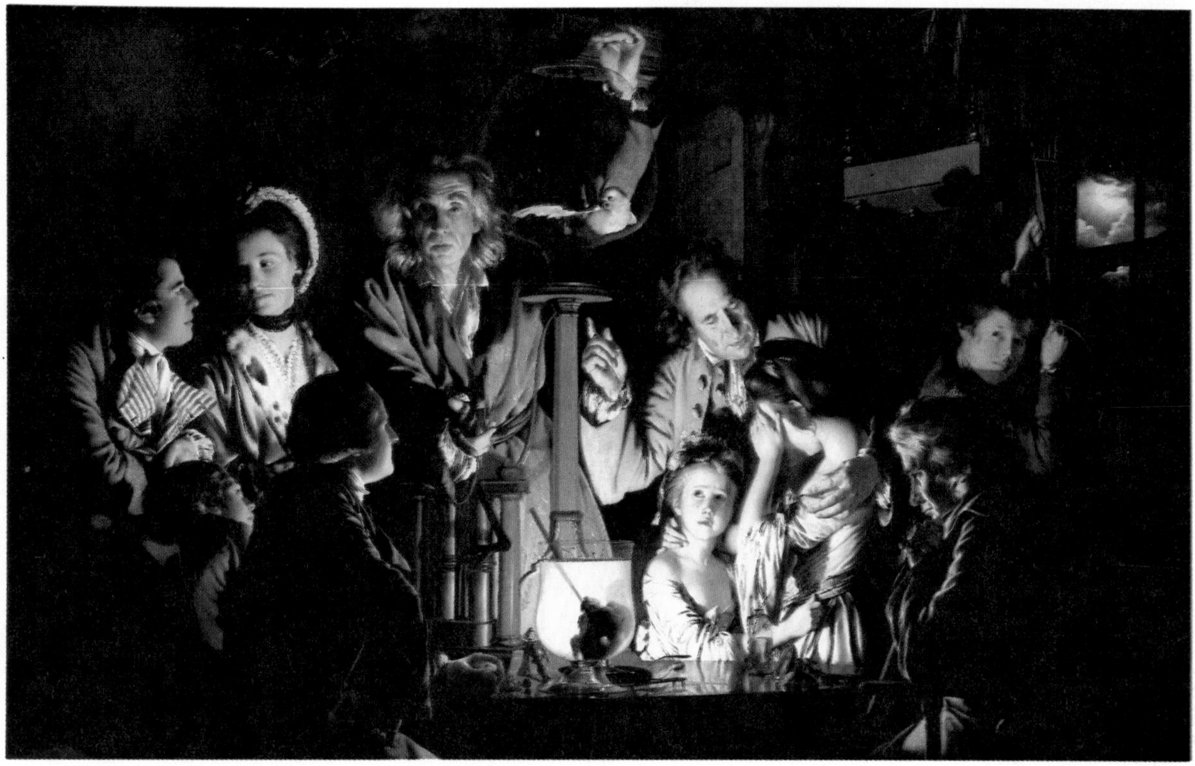

What Is Air?

The diagram shows that air is made up mostly of **nitrogen** gas, which our bodies cannot make use of. Air also contains oxygen, **carbon dioxide,** and other gases.

The air we breathe in contains more oxygen than the air we breathe out. Our bodies use the oxygen in the air to burn food which gives us **energy.** We breathe out carbon dioxide as a waste gas.

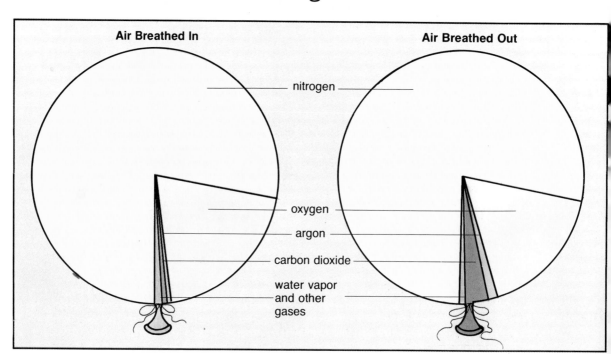

Air Breathed In

Air Breathed Out

nitrogen

oxygen

argon

carbon dioxide

water vapor and other gases

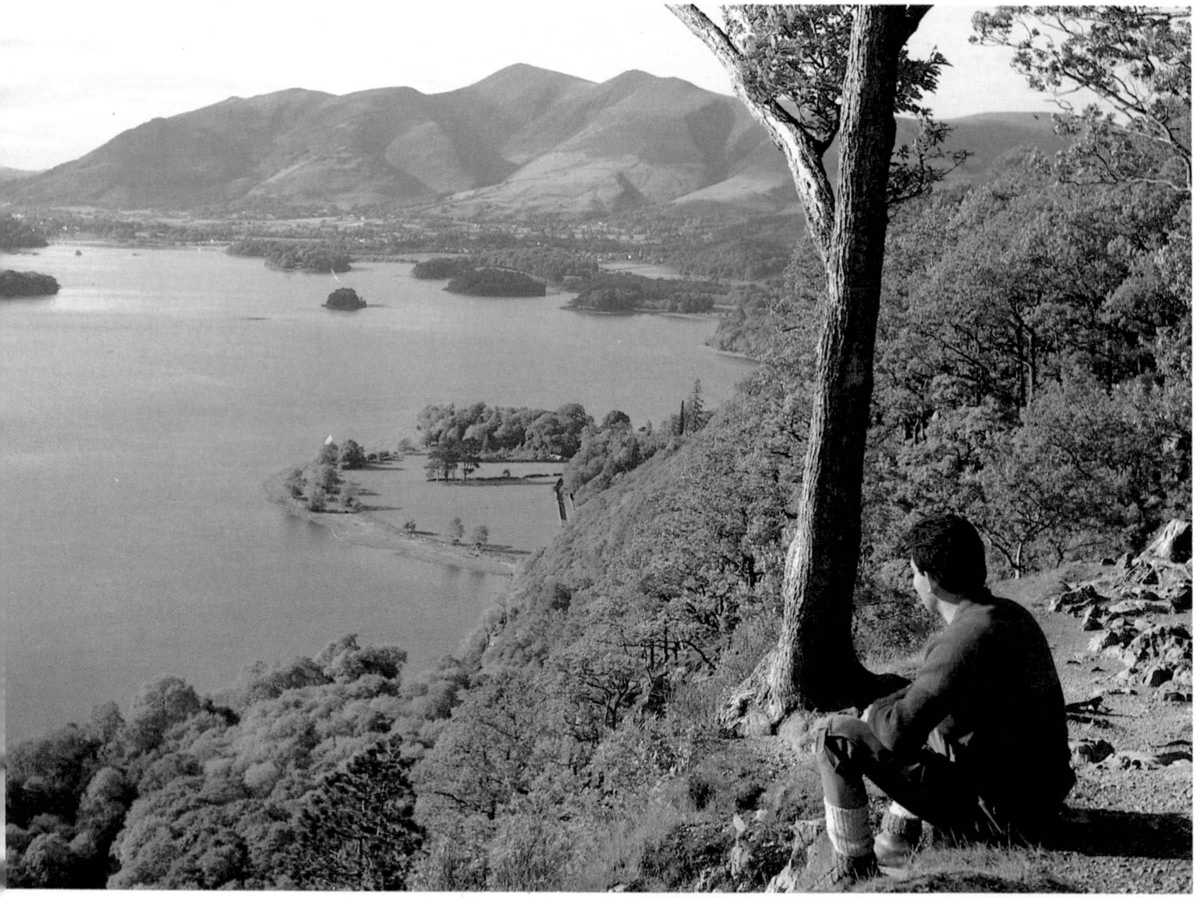

Green plants take in the carbon dioxide that we breathe out, making new oxygen to breathe in.

Cars and factories cause **pollution** which makes the air dirty and can harm our lungs.

the air over Los Angeles is heavily polluted

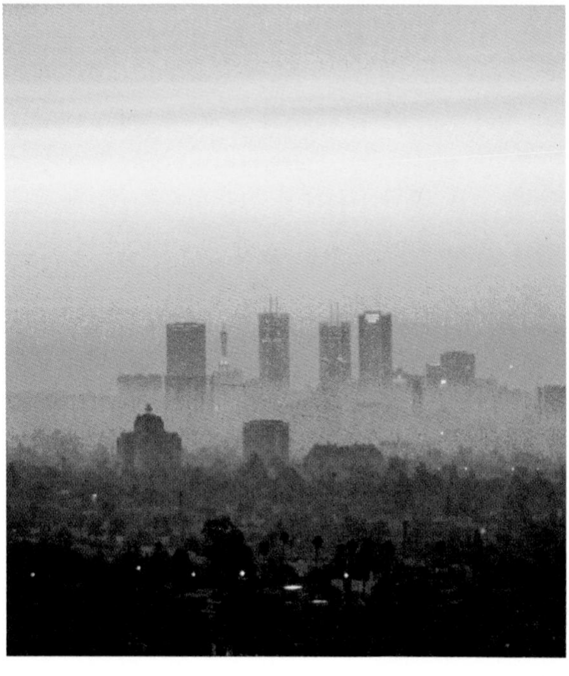

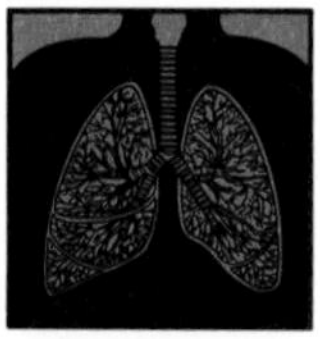

Why We Breathe

The photo, taken under a **microscope,** shows some of the tiny **cells** that make up your body. Each cell needs oxygen, which it gets through your **respiratory system.**

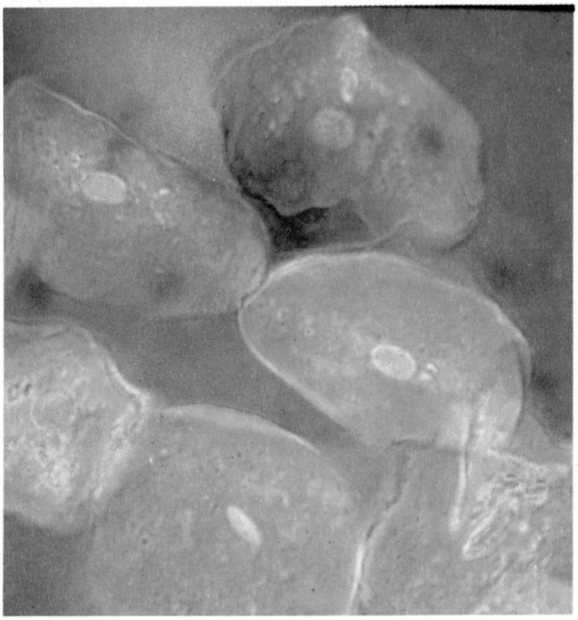

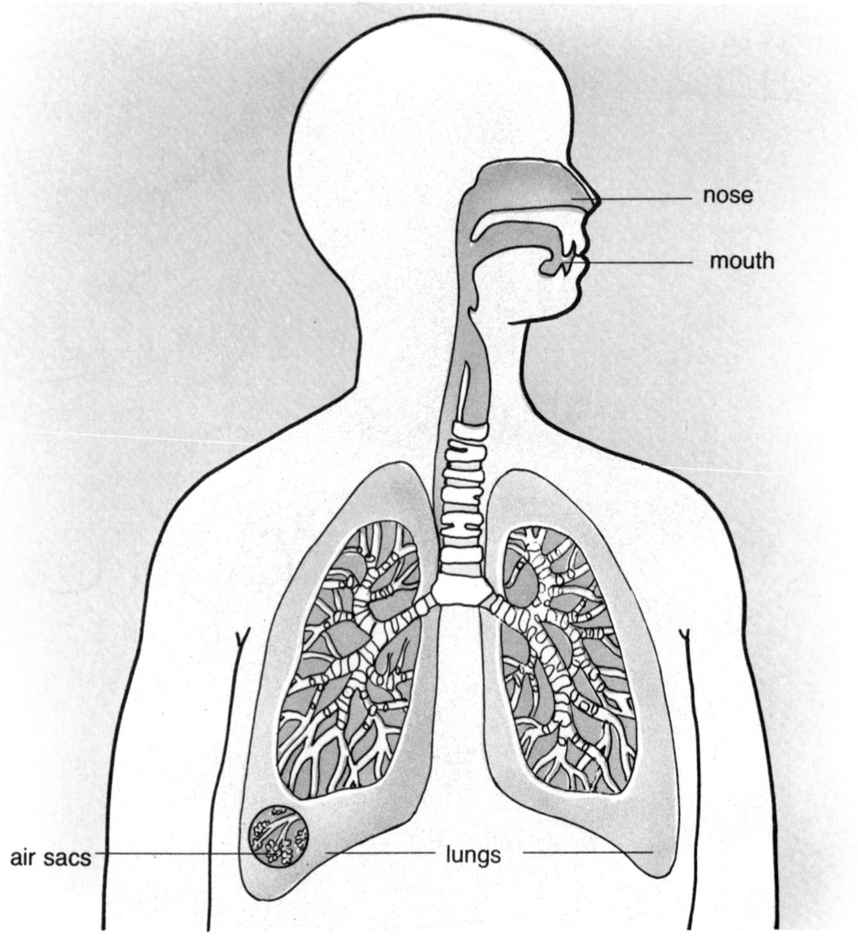
nose
mouth
air sacs
lungs

a diagram of your respiratory system

Air gets into your body through your nose and mouth, then it passes down your windpipe to thousands of tiny air sacs in your lungs.

Here, oxygen from the air is taken in by **red blood cells** inside the tubes that surround the lungs. These cells carry oxygen from the lungs to the heart, which pumps the oxygen-rich blood around your body.

red blood cells

Taking in Air

Your nose, mouth, and air passages in your throat are all linked together. This is why when you pick up **germs** from the air and catch a cold, you may have a runny nose, a dry mouth, and a sore throat.

nose
cavity
mouth
teeth
tongue
throat

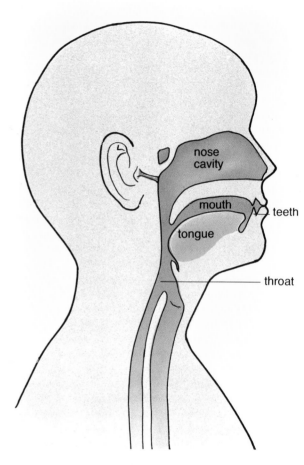

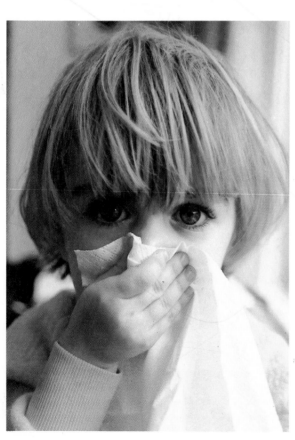

Your nose **cavity** is lined with a thin layer of skin. This produces a sticky **mucus** that collects dust and germs from the air. When you blow your nose, you get rid of this mucus and can breathe more easily.

Cells at the top of the nose cavity give us our sense of smell. There are about 15 different kinds of these cells.

They help us to recognize more than 3,000 different smells!

cells in the nose cavity pick up the scent of the rose

Air and Speech

The diagram shows how you make sounds. Inside your **larynx** are two **vocal cords,** which shake when air from your lungs passes between them.

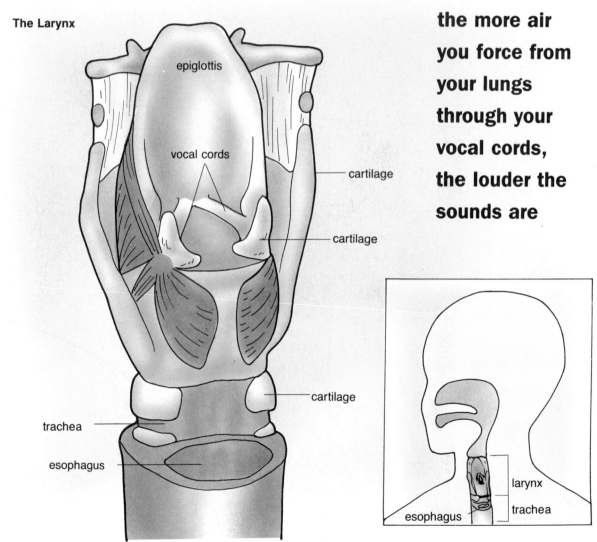

The Larynx

epiglottis

vocal cords

cartilage

cartilage

cartilage

trachea

esophagus

the more air you force from your lungs through your vocal cords, the louder the sounds are

larynx

trachea

esophagus

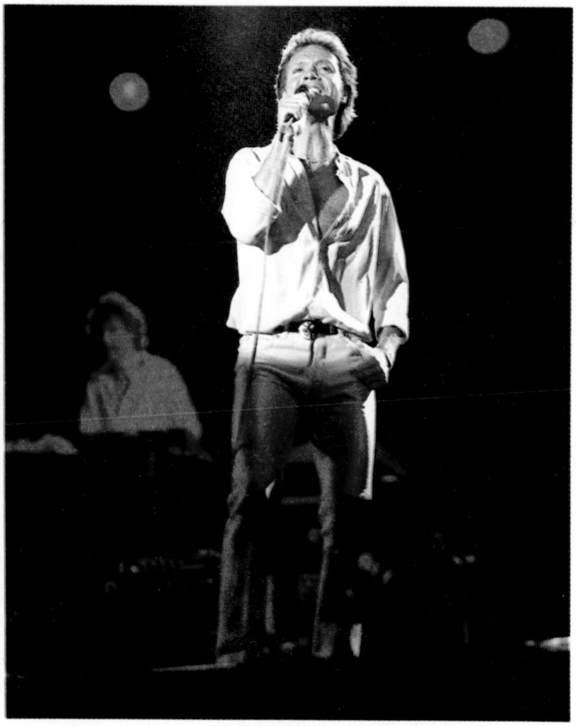

a singer or a baby crying makes sounds with the vocal cords in the larynx

If you touch your throat when you are speaking, you can feel your larynx at the top of your windpipe. Your vocal cords are attached to your larynx by strong, elastic tissue called **cartilage.** You make different sounds by making your vocal cords tighter or looser.

Your **epiglottis,** attached to your larynx, keeps food out of your windpipe.

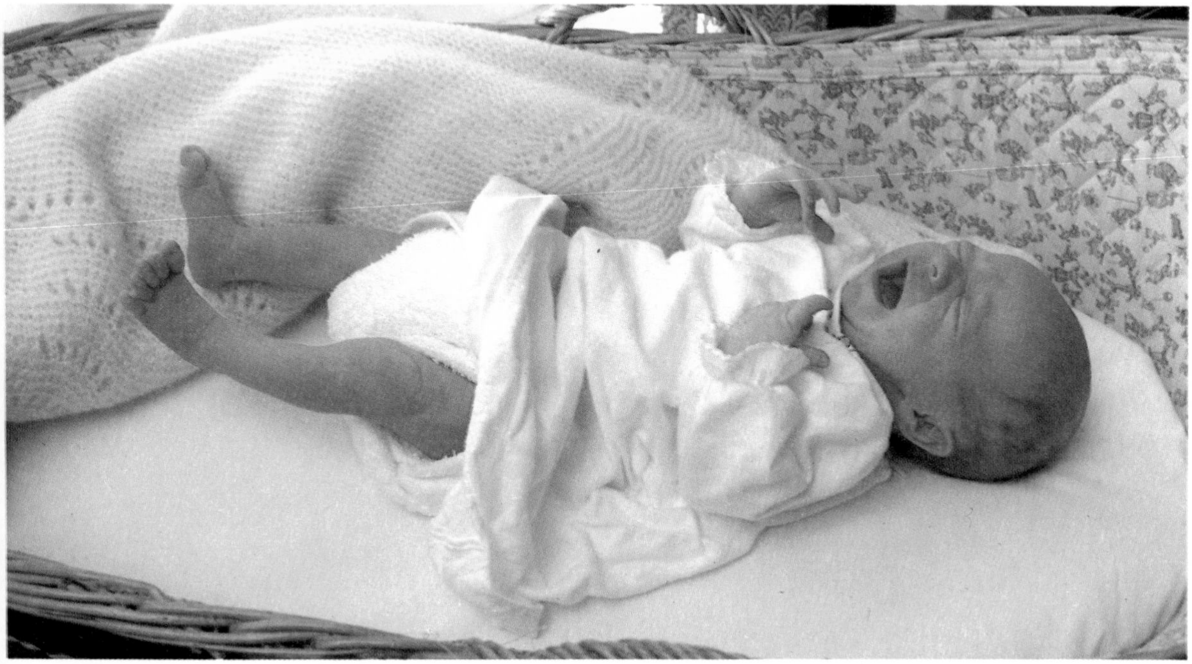

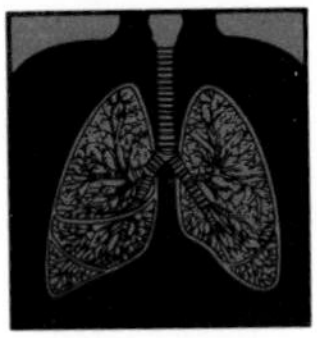

Into the Lungs

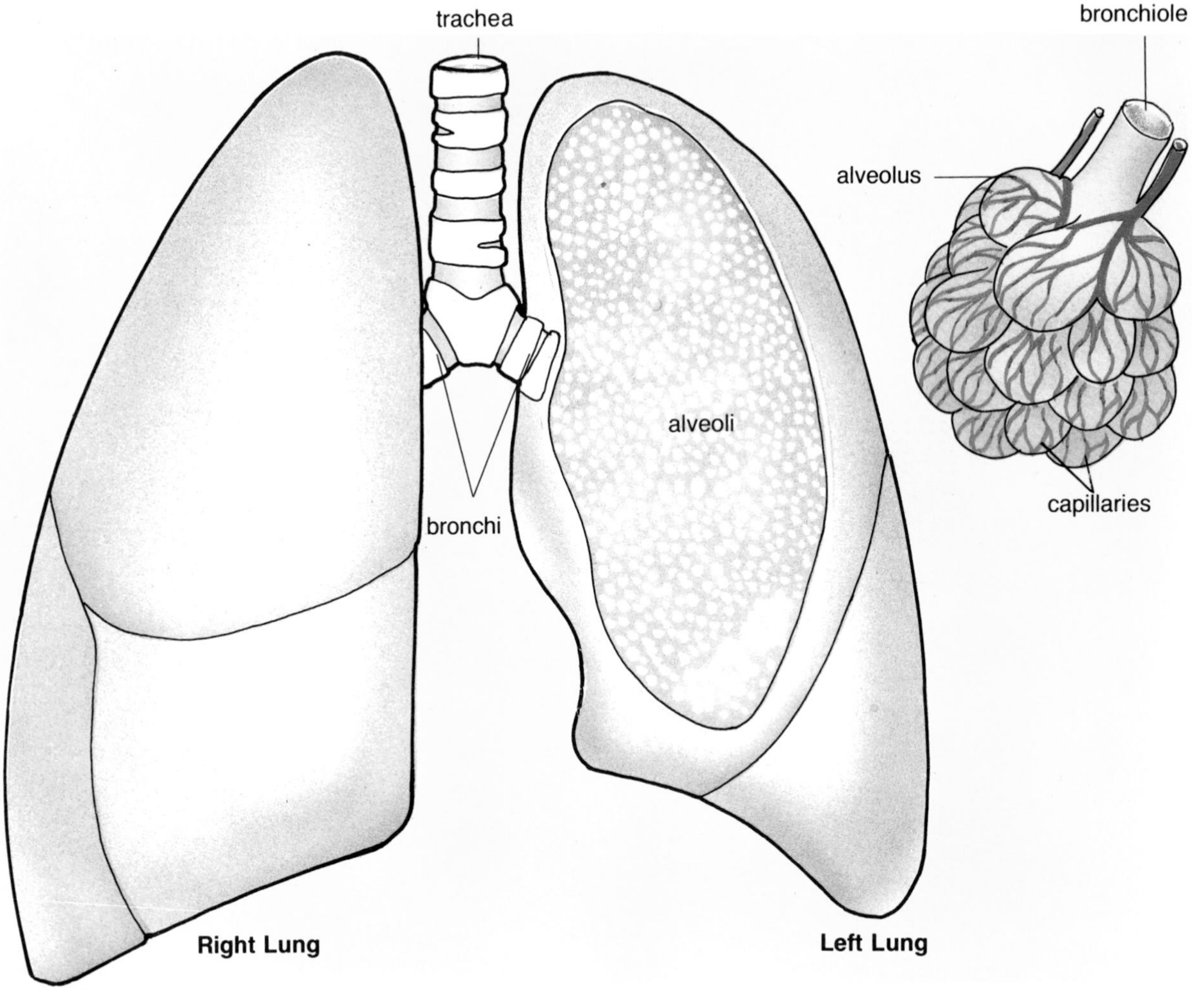
trachea
bronchiole
alveolus
alveoli
bronchi
capillaries
Right Lung
Left Lung

The lower end of the windpipe divides into **bronchi** which lead to each lung. The picture of the inside of the left lung shows a spongy mass made up of millions of air sacs or **alveoli.**

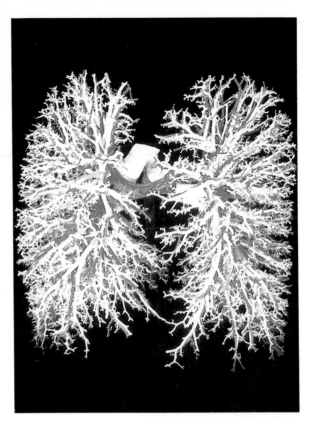

inside a lung, showing the passages of air in white and blood in red

Air enters the alveoli through the **bronchioles.** Each bronchiole ends in a bunch of alveoli. Every alveolus is covered with tiny **capillaries** which contain blood.

Tiny hairs called **cilia** inside the lungs protect them from dust.

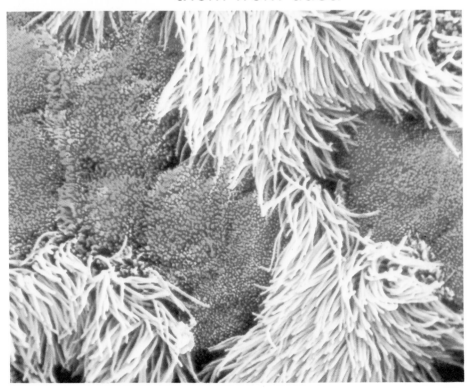

cilia look like grass blown by the wind

Into the Blood

Inside each alveolus, oxygen from the air is exchanged for carbon dioxide from the blood that the body has used.

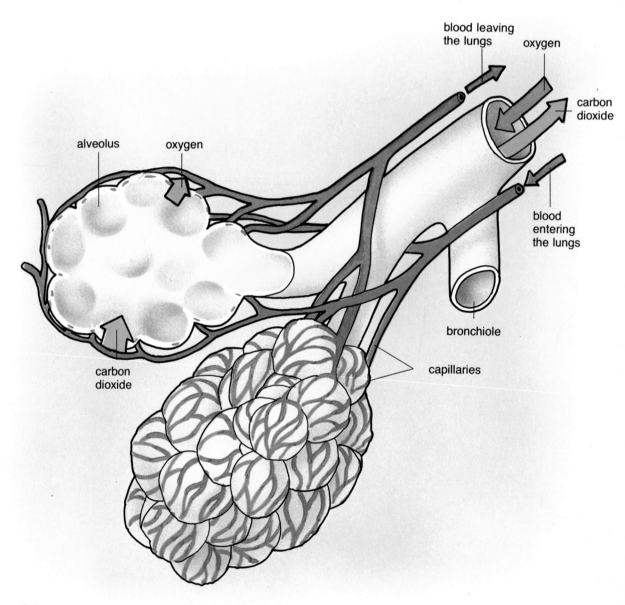

blood leaving the lungs

oxygen

carbon dioxide

alveolus

oxygen

blood entering the lungs

bronchiole

carbon dioxide

capillaries

Blood with oxygen from the lungs goes to your heart. Your heart pumps the blood around your body through your **arteries.**

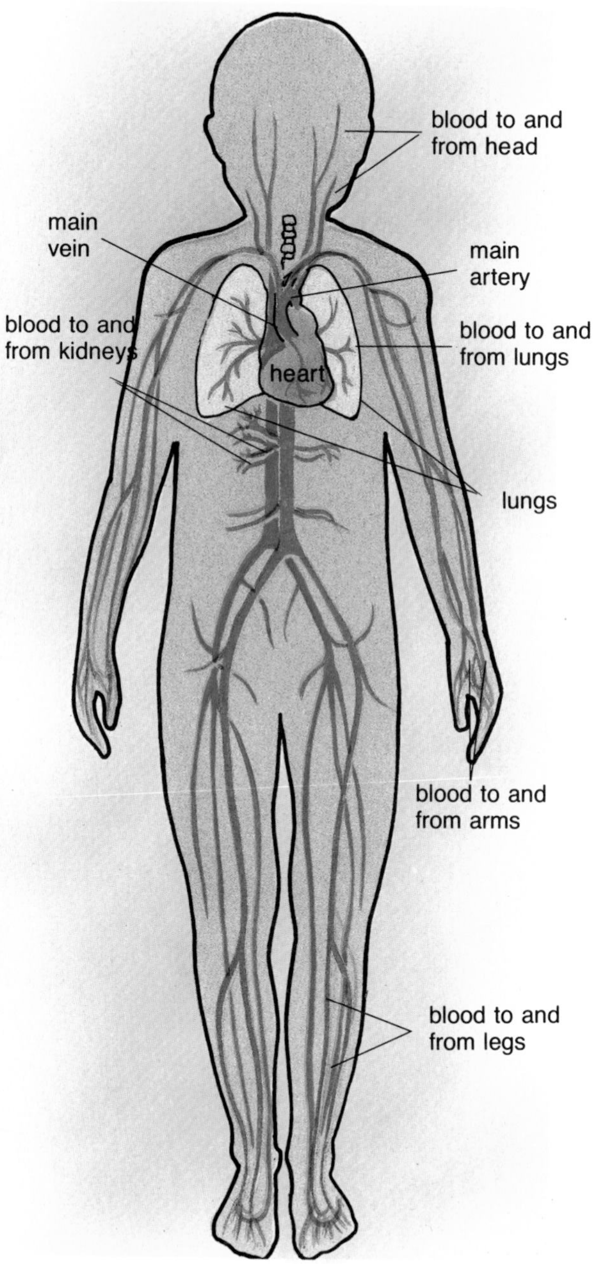

blood to and from head
main vein
main artery
blood to and from kidneys
blood to and from lungs
heart
lungs
blood to and from arms
blood to and from legs

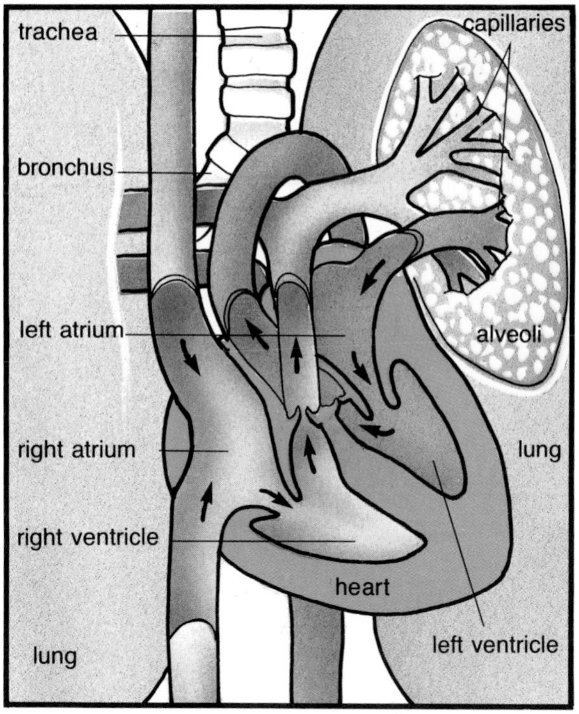

trachea
capillaries
bronchus
left atrium
alveoli
right atrium
lung
right ventricle
heart
lung
left ventricle

how your heart works

Your arteries branch into a network of tiny capillaries which pass the oxygen from your blood into the surrounding cells. A network of **veins** takes the stale blood with no oxygen in it back from these cells to your heart. Your heart then pumps this stale blood to your lungs to pick up more oxygen.

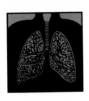

How the Lungs Work

Your lungs are covered by your **ribs.**
When you breathe in, **muscles** in your
diaphragm flatten and pull downward
and air is pulled into your lungs.
When you breathe out, the muscles
relax, your diaphragm moves upward,
and air is pushed out.

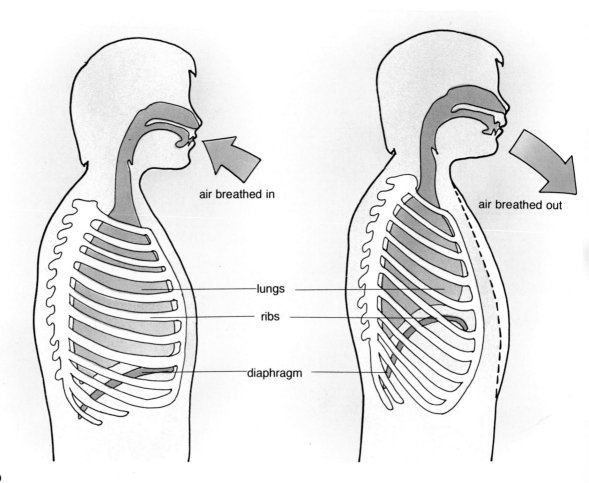

air breathed in

air breathed out

lungs

ribs

diaphragm

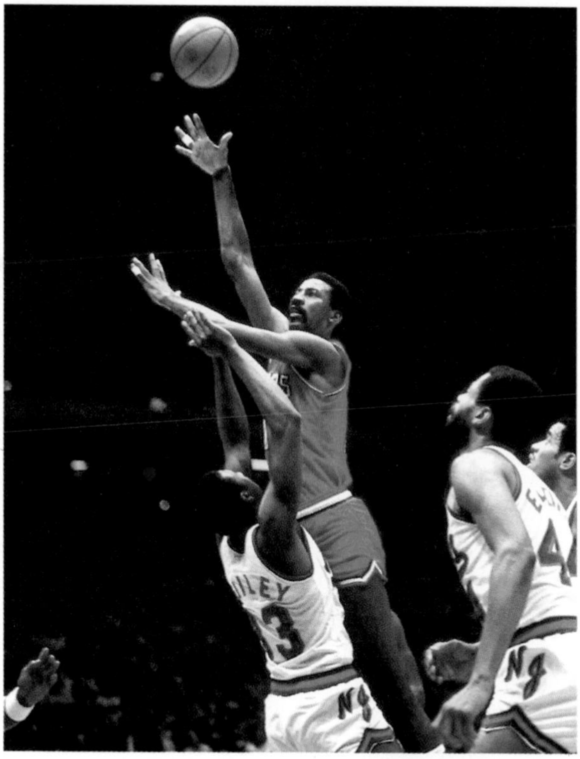

Your lungs hold about the same amount of air as a party balloon.

When you are breathing quietly, you take between 15 and 20 breaths each minute to draw in air. When you exercise, your muscles need more oxygen, so you breathe faster and deeper and your heart beats much faster.

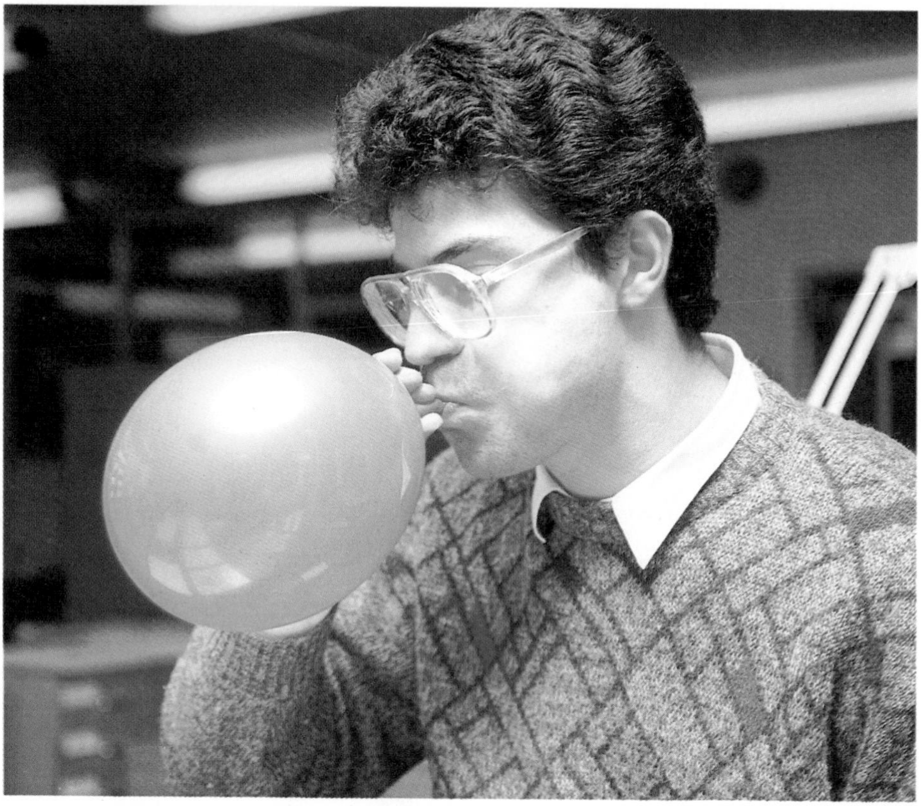

you cannot blow up a balloon in one breath because some air always stays in the lungs

Sneezing and Yawning

You sneeze if something tickles your nose. Sneezing and coughing clears the air passages.

The photograph shows the **particles** made by a sneeze. These particles contain germs, so when you sneeze, always use a handkerchief or turn away.

yawning pulls in air

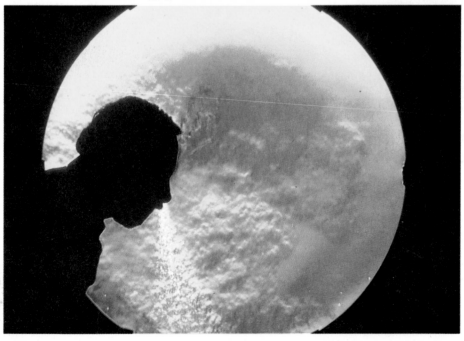

sneezing spreads germs

We yawn when we are tired or bored or if the room is very stuffy. A yawn seems to be the body's way of getting more oxygen in order to make us feel more lively. During a yawn, the air is sucked into your lungs and then released.

The air you breathe out contains quite a lot of water **vapor.** On a cold day you can see the vapor in the air in front of your face.

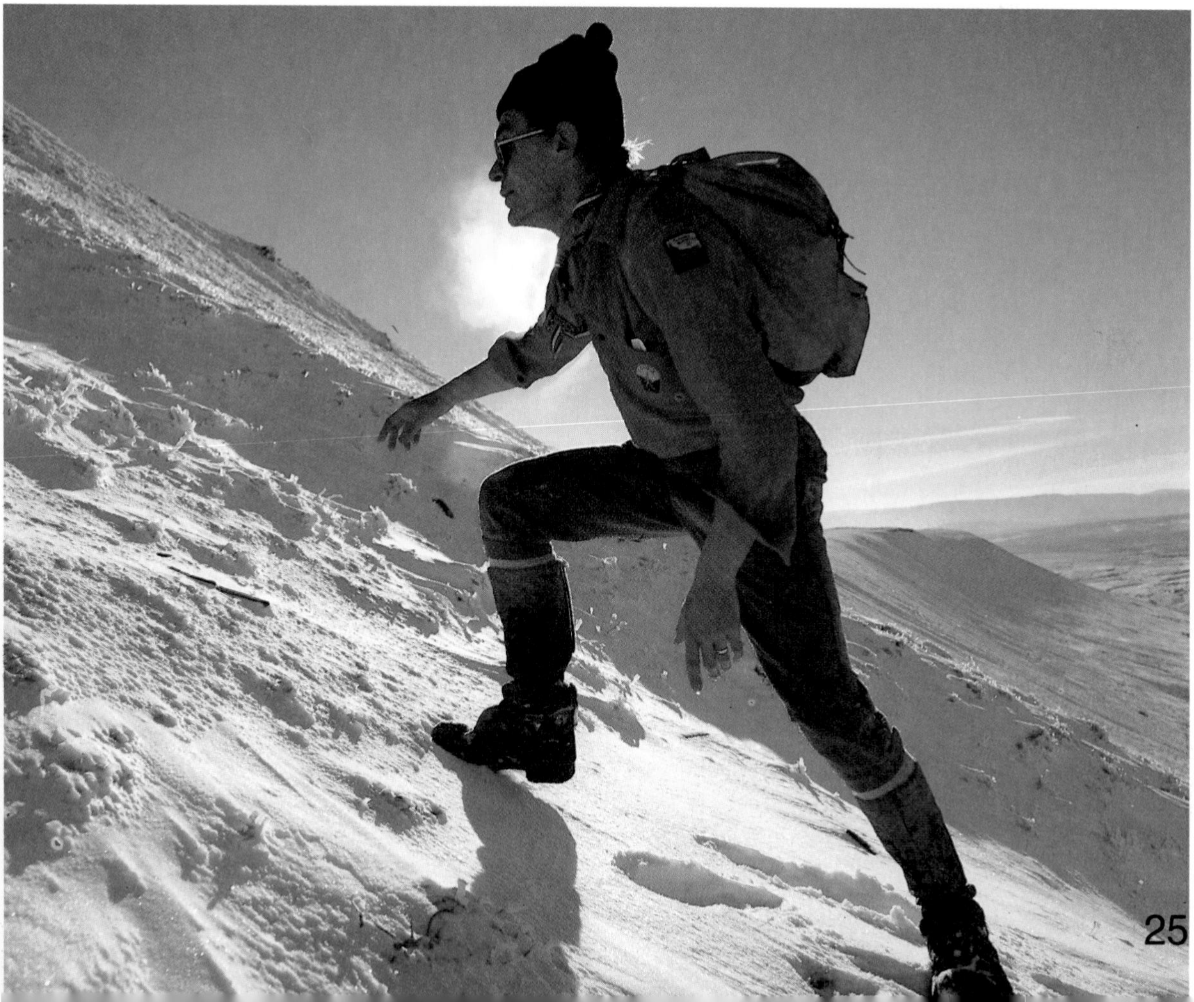

Checking the Lungs

The doctor in the picture is using a **stethoscope** to listen to the air as it moves in and out of the child's lungs.

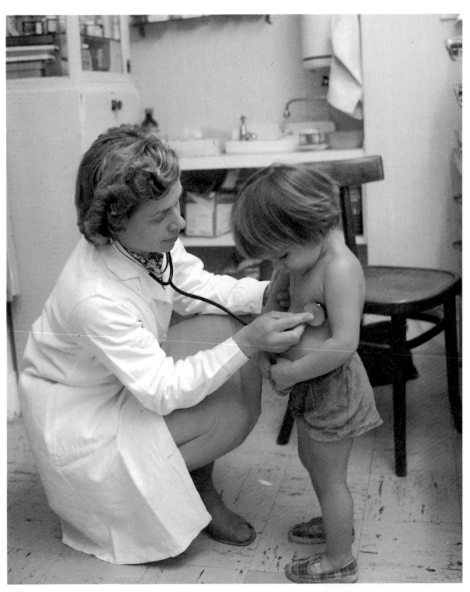

taking an X-ray photograph

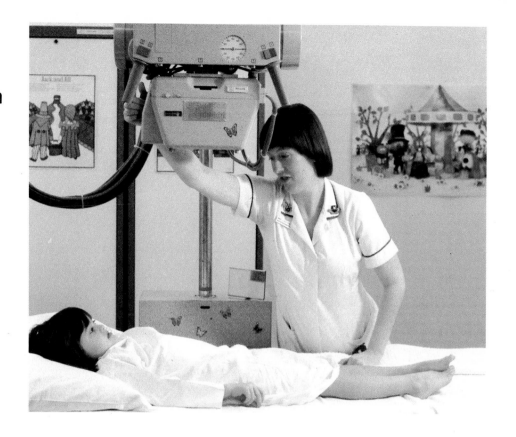

Doctors can tell if there is anything wrong with your lungs by the sounds of your breathing. Squeaking, creaking, or whistling noises could be a sign of **infection.** Doctors can also look at **X-ray** photographs of your chest and lungs to see if your lungs are infected.

an X-ray photograph of a patient's chest

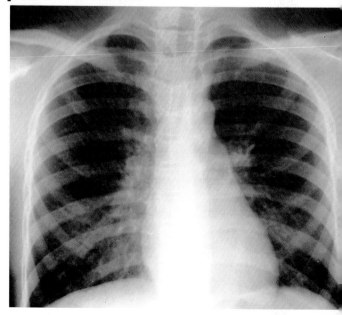

Breathing Problems

Many people get **hay fever** because they are **allergic** to pollen dust.

you can see the pollen dust falling from these catkins

using a spray helps this child breathe more easily

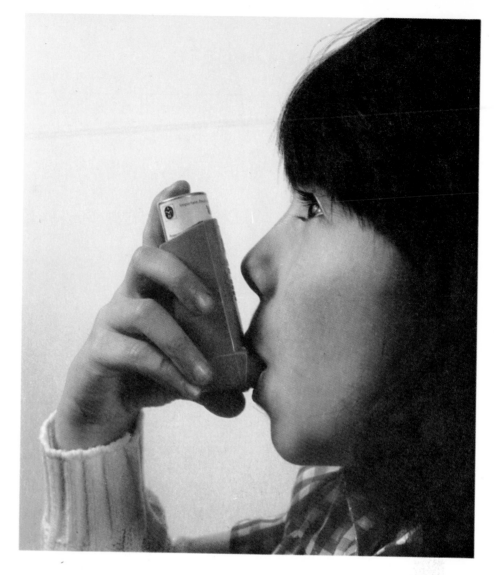

Other people suffer from **asthma.** The bronchioles of their lungs become **inflamed** and swollen and breathing is difficult.

A spray often helps relax the muscles of the bronchioles and allows air to flow easily into the lungs.

Fighting Disease

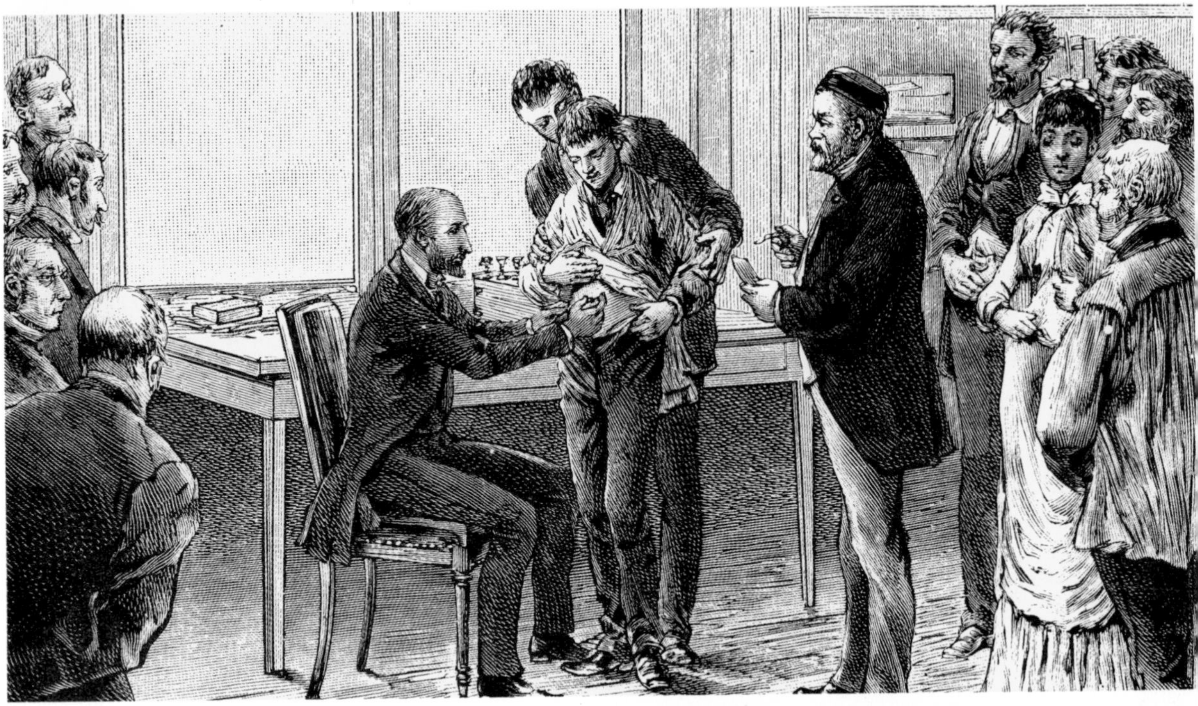

The picture shows Louis Pasteur, the first person to discover that germs cause disease.

Today we also know that breathing in chemical sprays can harm the lungs. This man wears a mask to cover his mouth and nose when he sprays crops.

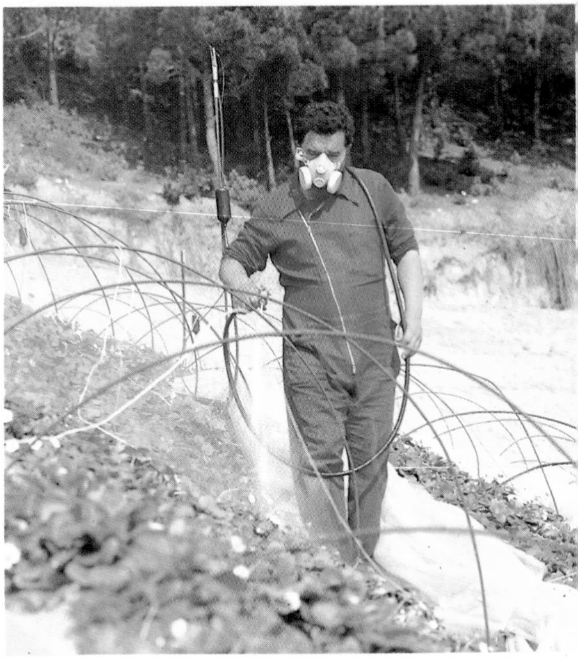

The most serious disease of the lungs is **cancer,** when cells in the lung tissue start to divide rapidly and form a lump of cancer cells. If cancer is not treated, it spreads and the lung can become too badly damaged to work.

Tuberculosis is a disease of the lungs that is not as common today as it was a hundred years ago. The boy in this photograph is being tested for tuberculosis. He can be **vaccinated** against it.

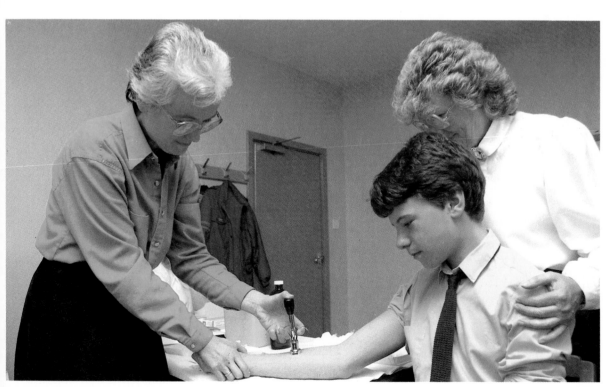

Treatments Today

Doctors can help people with lung diseases. The machine on the right measures how hard the girl can blow and shows if her lungs are working properly. If they are not, a machine called a **ventilator** can be used to help her breathe.

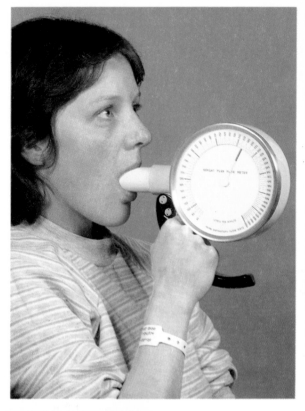

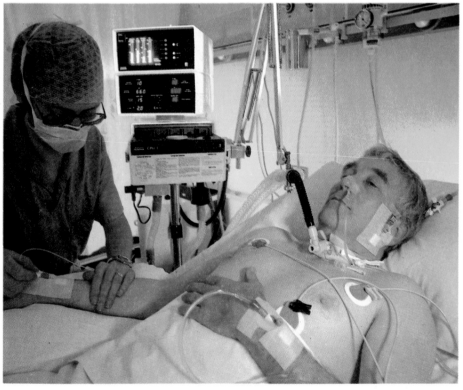

ventilators draw air into the lungs and check the amount and pressure of the air

testing for different allergies

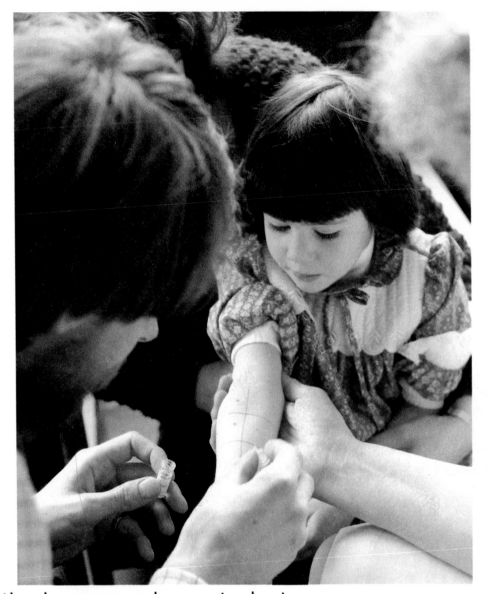

If the lungs need a rest, doctors can use an **artificial lung** to take their place and put oxygen in the blood.

Doctors can also do tests for many different allergies. The child in this picture is being tested to see what she is allergic to.

Operations

When **surgeons** operate, they cut through the skin, muscles, and **nerves,** and the patient feels pain. In the past, doctors tried different plants and drugs to make the pain less. Then surgeons began to use **anesthetics** to stop the patient from feeling pain. Breathing in certain gases made the patient feel relaxed and sleepy.

Today patients are given a drug to make them sleepy. This may be followed by a mixture of gases.

gas made a patient sleepy

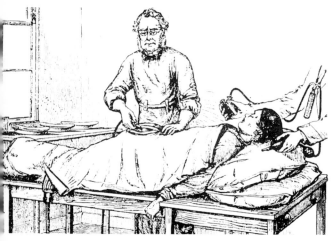

the root of a mandrake was used to make people relax

34

The **anesthetist** in the picture decides which drugs to give a patient before and during an operation. She makes sure the patient is asleep and continues breathing.

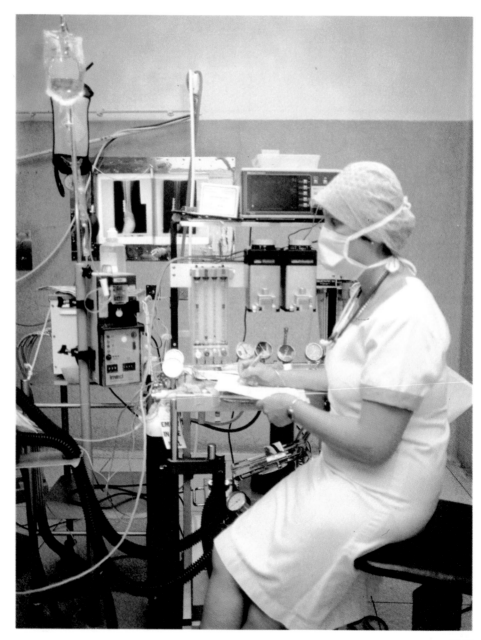

this anesthetist checks the amount of drugs during an operation

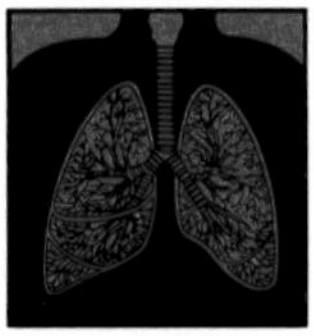

To the Rescue

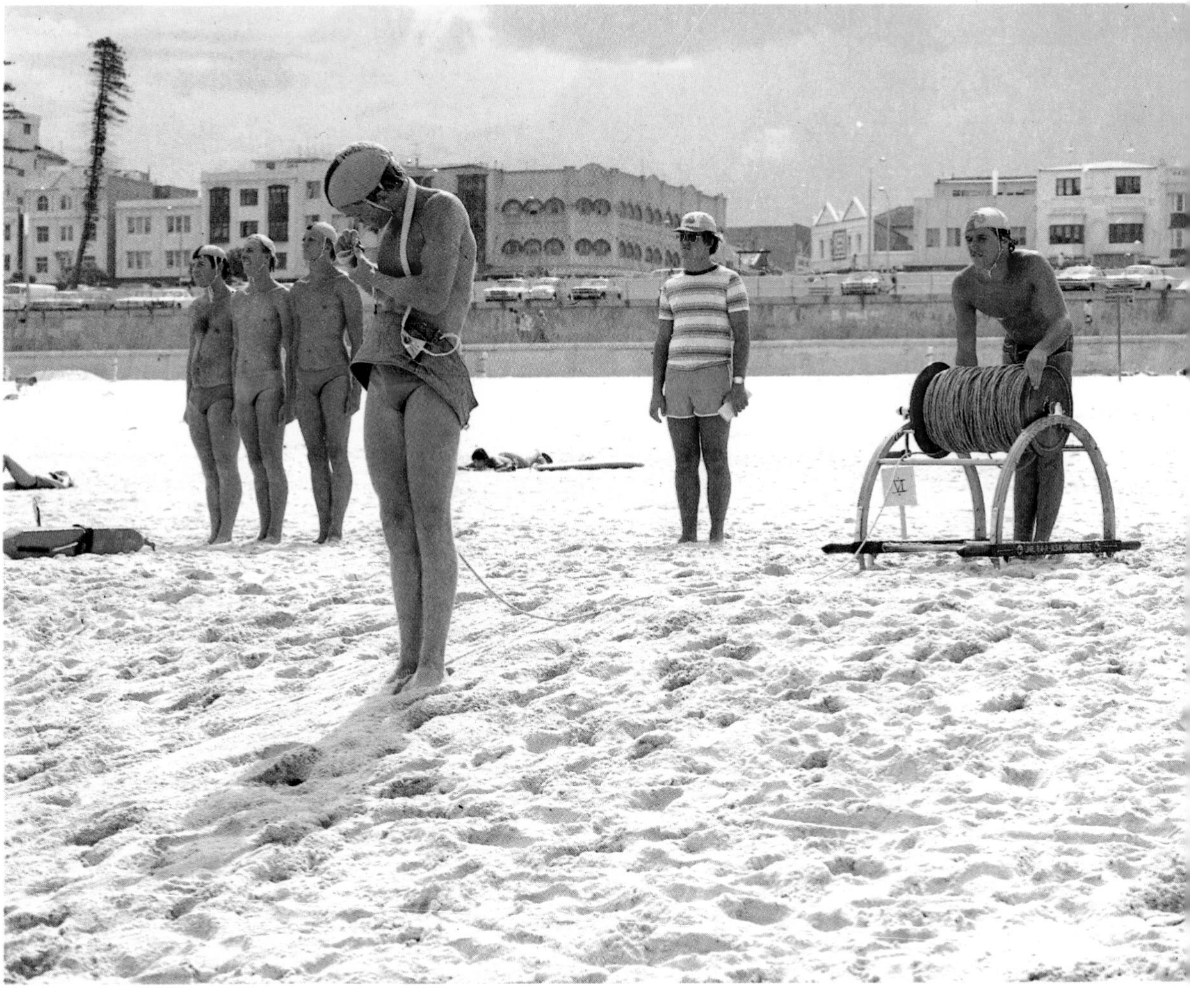

These lifeguards on an Australian beach save people who are drowning. They are also trained in first aid. Groups like the Red Cross run courses to teach people first aid.

If a person stops breathing, he or she must be made to start breathing again, quickly. Only those trained in first aid should give the kiss of life to someone who has stopped breathing.

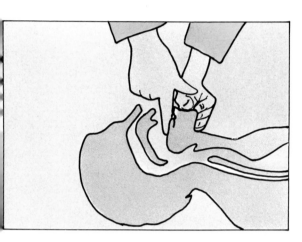

the throat is checked to see if it is blocked by the tongue

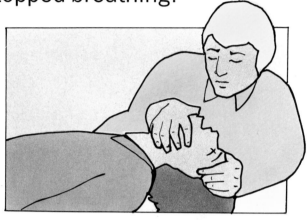

the head is tipped back, the nose held, and breathing is forced into the mouth

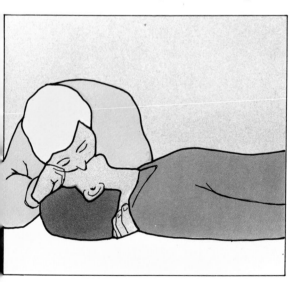

four quick breaths are given, then 16 a minute

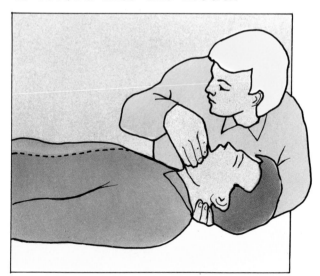

the chest is checked to see if it is rising and falling

Keeping Fit

Your muscles need a constant supply of oxygen when you exercise, so you have to breathe deeply and often. This makes your breathing muscles strong and increases the amount of air you can take into your lungs. Regular exercise strengthens both your heart and your lungs.

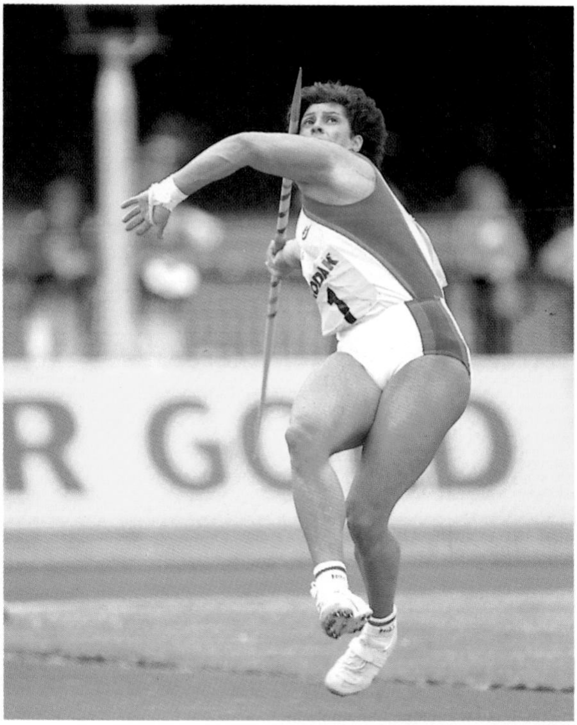
R GO D

Short bursts of exercise are not as good for you as longer-lasting exercise, like cycling and swimming.

Throwing the javelin needs a lot of strength and skill. It uses a short burst of energy, but this kind of exercise does not help your body take in much oxygen.

a bicycle ride in the fresh air gives us oxygen to keep our muscles working well

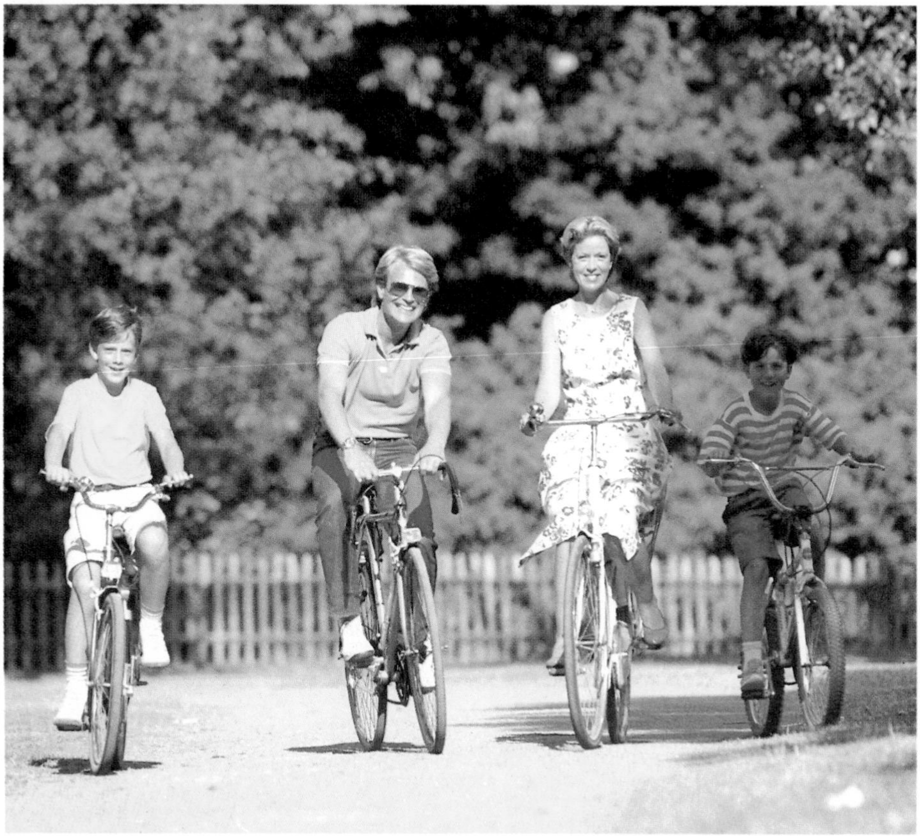

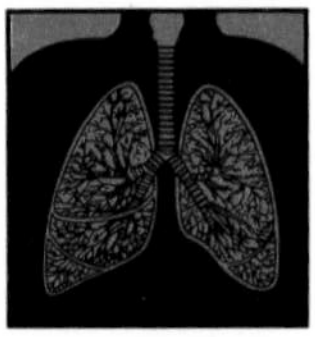

Breathing Deeply

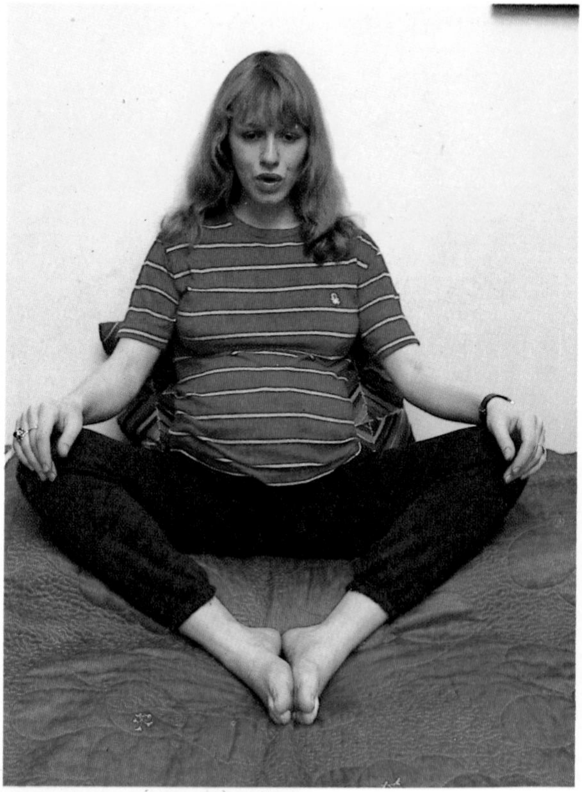

Breathing correctly is good for your health.

The woman in this photo is learning breathing exercises which will help her keep calm and relaxed during her baby's birth.

Singers also learn how to breathe very deeply.

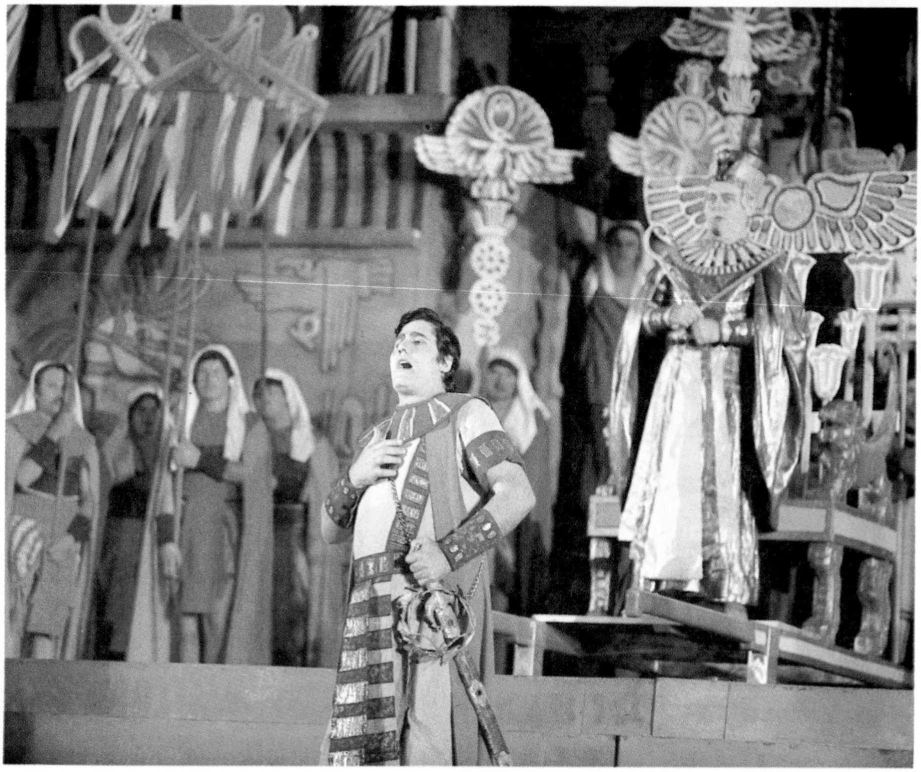

a singer must breathe deeply

this man is learning from his yoga teacher how to breathe deeply

Breathing control is a very important part of yoga.

You should learn to breathe in through your nose and out through your mouth. The nose filters out dust and germs before they reach the lungs.

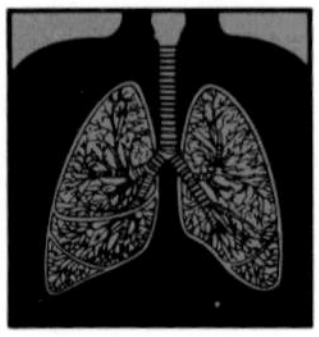

Smoking and Health

The man in the picture is suffering from a disease caused by smoking cigarettes. He has to wear a special mask to help him breathe.

A person who does not smoke is likely to live 15 or 20 years longer than a person who does smoke.

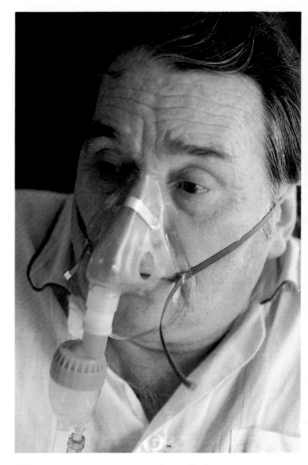

Cigarette smoke blown through a handkerchief leaves behind a smear of brown tar. This is what smokers breathe into their lungs. Tar spreads over the layer of skin lining the air passages and lungs. It makes them swollen and can lead to a disease called **bronchitis.**

If the cilia that help get rid of germs get covered in tar from cigarette smoke, they cannot do their job of keeping the lungs clean. In many cases this leads to cancer of the lungs, throat, or mouth.

Many countries have banned cigarette advertising on TV and do not allow smoking in public places.

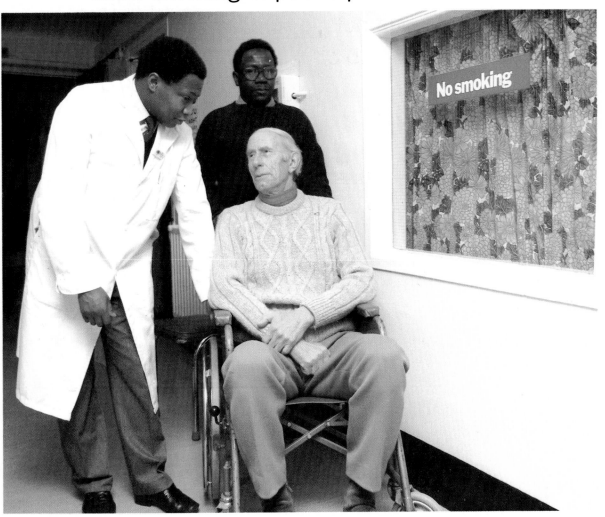

New Worlds

When this scuba diver explores a coral reef, he breathes in air from the tanks on his back.

Humans cannot live in places where there is no air to breathe. We cannot breathe under water and we cannot live in space. We need special equipment in both cases.

Astronauts who travel in space carry an air supply with them. Outside the spaceship they wear spacesuits and breathe oxygen from bottles they carry on their backs.

Perhaps one day we shall build huge spaceships with their own supply of air. People could live and breathe in them and grow plants to make more oxygen.

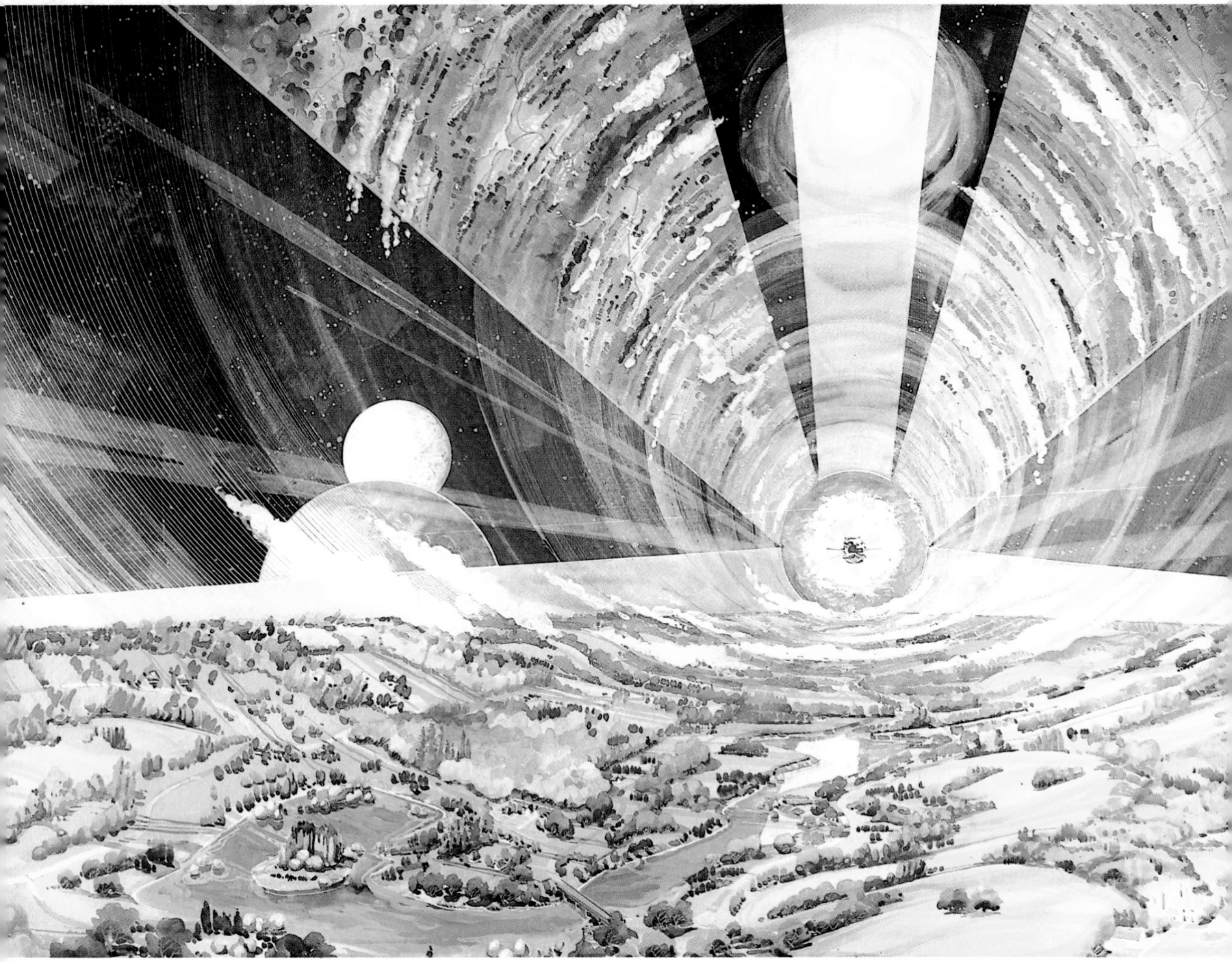

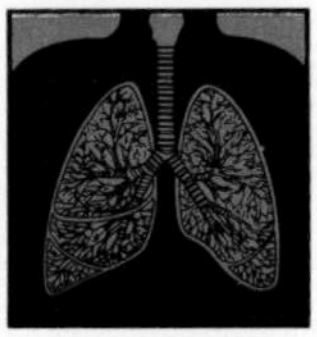

Glossary

allergic a reaction to something such as dust that causes illness.

alveoli the tiny pockets of air that make up your lungs.

anesthetic something that makes people lose their sense of pain or feeling.

anesthetist the person in a hospital who makes sure that a patient does not feel any pain during an operation.

artery one of the main tubes that carry fresh blood from your heart to parts of the body.

artificial lung a machine used to take air into and out of the blood when the lungs are not working.

asthma an illness that makes it difficult to breathe properly.

bronchi the two breathing tubes joined to the lungs.

bronchioles the breathing tubes that carry air inside the lungs.

bronchitis an illness when the tubes taking air to the lungs become swollen and sore.

cancer a very serious disease that can attack the lungs.

capillary one of a network of tiny tubes that carry blood to and from parts of the body.

carbon dioxide a gas made of carbon and oxygen.

cartilage a tough, rubbery material found in some parts of the body.

cavity a space inside something.

cell a very small part of a unit.

cilia tiny hairs that grow in parts of the body such as breathing tubes.

diaphragm a flat sheet of muscle under your lungs.

elements the basic materials from which everything in the universe is made.

energy the power to do work.

epiglottis a flap of tissue behind the tongue that closes over the top of the windpipe when you swallow.

germ a tiny living thing that can cause disease.

gills the part of a water animal that is used for breathing.

hay fever the sneezing and watering of the eyes that happens to some people when they breathe in pollen.

infection an invasion of part of a body by a germ.

inflamed to be swollen and feel hot and sore.

larynx the part of the throat that we use to make sounds.

lungs the two sponge-like body parts used to breathe.

mammals animals that give birth to live young and feed them with mother's milk.

microscope an instrument that makes tiny things look larger.

mucus a clear, sticky substance produced by the lining of some parts of the body.

muscle a type of material in the body that can shorten itself to produce movement.

nerve part of a network of tiny "cables" that pass messages from all parts of the body to the brain.

nitrogen a gas found in living things and in the air.

oxygen a gas found in air and water. We cannot breathe without oxygen.

particles very small pieces or drops.

pollution anything that dirties or poisons air, land, or water.

pressure the action of something pressing on, or against, something.

red blood cells cells that carry oxygen.

respiratory system the parts of an animal used for breathing.

ribs a series of long bones that form a cage around the heart and lungs.

stethoscope an instrument that a doctor uses to listen to the sounds in your body made by the heart and lungs.

surgeon a doctor who treats illness and injuries by operating on the body.

tuberculosis a disease that causes the lungs to become covered in small lumps.

vaccination a dose of specially treated germs strong enough for the body to learn to protect itself against them.

vapor a liquid that forms tiny drops in the air when heated.

vein a main tube that carries stale blood from all over the body to the heart and lungs.

ventilator a machine that pumps air in and out of a person's body.

vocal cords the two thin bands found in the throat that shake when air passes over them. Your vocal cords control what your voice sounds like.

windpipe the tube that goes between the throat and the lungs to carry air to the lungs.

X ray a ray that can see through solid objects.

Index

© Heinemann Children's Reference 1990
Artwork © BLA Publishing Limited 1987

Material used in this book first appeared in Macmillan World Library: *How Our Bodies Work: The Lungs and Breathing.* Published by Heinemann Children's Reference.

Photographic credits
(t = top b = bottom l = left r = right)
cover: © Four By Five/Superstock
4 Frank Lane Picture Library; 5 Horace Dobbs; 6 Bridgeman Colour Library; 8 Ann Ronan Picture Library; 9 National Gallery; 11*t* J. Allan Cash; 11*b* ZEFA; 12, 13 Science Photo Library; 14, 15 Vision International; 17*t* J. Allan Cash; 17*b* S. & R. Greenhill; 18*t*, 18*b* Science Photo Library; 23 Trevor Hill; 24*t* Vision International; 24*b* Science Photo Library; 25 Chris Fairclough Picture Library; 26 S. & R. Greenhill; 27*t* Vision International; 27*b*, 28, 29 Science Photo Library; 30*t* Vivien Fifield; 30*b* Frank Lane Picture Agency; 31 S. & R. Greenhill; 32*b* Science Photo Library; 33 Vision International; 34*l* Science Photo Library; 34*r* Ann Ronan Picture Library; 35 Science Photo Library; 36 J. Allan Cash; 38, 39*t* Sporting Pictures; 39 ZEFA; 40*t* S. & R. Greenhill; 40*b* ZEFA; 41 Science Photo Library; 42*t* S. & R. Greenhill; 42*b* Vision International; 43 Trevor Hill; 44, 45 Science Photo Library